BEEKMAN HILLS

KC ENDERS

Visit my website at www.kcenderswrites.com
Cover Designer: Alyssa Garcia, Uplifting Author Services
Editor: Jovana Shirley, Unforeseen Editing, www.unforeseenediting.com
Proofreader: Judy Zweifel, Judy's Proofreading

ISBN-13: 979-8431466861

Twist

BEEKMAN HILLS

To my 'fiends'
I wouldn't be doing this without you.
Thank you.

1

"ARE YOU AN ANGEL FROM HEAVEN?"

"NO. SATAN LET ME OUT IN COSTUME TODAY."

Adelaide

People suck. I mean, not all people, but having to meet with them and listen to their "creative ideas" on what they want on their websites is the least favorite part of my job.

God, and having to meet with them out in public? Where there are people? I am not Ariel. I do not want to be where the people are. It takes everything I have in me not to roll my eyes. I need to be professional and land this job.

I creep down Main Street, cursing the plows for not doing any kind of a decent job of clearing the snow from the roads. Maybe my anger is misplaced because Mother Nature should have checked with me before dumping a foot of snow overnight. The four and a half years I've spent here in New York for college have done nothing to put me at ease while driving in the snow. It snowed in Kansas City, but nothing like it does here.

The snow grabs at my tires, pushing my car toward the one other car on the road, coming from the opposite direction.

Shit, shit, shit, shit.

The car swerves across the road, cutting in front of me just as my tires catch, and I barely get things under control. I seethe every curse I can think of at the snow, the plows, the universe, and the asshole who almost hit me and made me miss my turn. And, now, I'm going to be late.

Twenty minutes later, after turning around, getting stuck in stupid one-way streets, and finally getting back to Main, I gingerly pull into the parking lot of McBride's. This is my first time actually going to the Irish pub in the almost four and a half years I've been in New York. With the millions of stories I'd heard throughout college about the pub and the whorish Irish guys working here, I'd have been fine with not coming at all.

With my messenger bag slung across my body, I shove my hands into my pockets and hurry to the door. I should know better; I really should. Just as I start to stomp the snow off my boots, my bag shifts and pulls me off-balance. Arms wheeling through the air, hands reaching for anything to stop the madness, I lose it. Bust ass and end up flat on my back in the snow bank to the left of the door.

Late.

Cold.

Ass covered in snow.

I'm so not getting this job. The wind whips my magenta-and-pale-pink hair up into a twirl of gourmet cotton-candy mess. I haul myself up and dust the snow off my black leggings, cringing when a chunk of snow finds its way into my boot. I don't have time for this. I should be home, cozy in my apartment, with some coffee and a blankie.

Small favors, but my glasses stayed on, and my computer is okay. Carefully, I get myself together, inhaling deeply and slapping what I hope is more smile than grimace on my face, and step into the pub.

The door slams shut behind me on a gust of wind, and all heads turn to face me. I clear my throat and approach the tall, dark-haired guy, pretty sure he's the photographer whose website I'm supposed to be building. "Mr. Kearney?"

"I am. Please, call me Aidan. Are you Miss Huntington?"

He reaches out to shake my hand, so I grit my teeth and firmly clasp his. Yeah, I don't like touching strangers either. They can have all kinds of germs. Like, how do you know if a person just picked their nose right before shaking your hand? His hand feels smooth and clean, so I hope for the best. Maybe I can discreetly grab my hand sanitizer as I unpack my computer.

"Adelaide," I tell him, following suit. "Great, so what are you looking for with your website?"

I really want to just get this started and done, so I can go home and hang out with Eric. He's the best roommate I could have ever asked for after living in the dorms for the first couple of years of school.

Aidan pauses and rests his hand on the back of the chair across from me. "Erm, I don't know really. I thought, with you being the expert, I'd let you guide me."

More small favors. Maybe this won't suck.

"Can I get you something to drink? A pint maybe?"

I stare at him for a second, not quite sure what to say. Is it professional to drink while working? Not that it matters. I don't really drink.

"I'll just have some coffee, I think. Thanks."

"You're sure?" His voice is deep, the accent a little more pronounced than when we spoke on the phone.

I nod and watch as he makes his way to the bar.

He grabs a tall glass of dark beer for himself and a steaming mug of coffee for me. "Do you take anything with it? Some sugar? Creamer?"

"Fuck's sake, I'm sure she doesn't need any sugar. She looks sweet and lovely to me." The bartender comes out of the back room with a basket of French fries, a cheesy smile stretched across his face. "She radiates sunshine and sweetness."

Dear God and sweet baby Jesus, help me have the strength not to roll my eyes. Please, please—

Obviously, those little prayers just did nothing for me. Aidan and the older guy sitting at the bar each bark out a loud laugh. And there goes my attempt to be professional.

"Just creamer, thanks," I tell Aidan.

Scowling, I turn back to my computer and pull my hair up into a messy bun, securing it with a couple of pens. The feet screech against the floor as I shift my chair in. I pull my feet up and wiggle around until I'm sitting crisscrossed on the hard wooden seat. I tuck a third pen between my lips and start typing, pulling up the site template. It would be great if he just gave me creative license, but we'll see. People say that shit all the time and then change every last detail on their sites.

"And look at how she folds herself up so neatly on that chair. She's sweet and bendy, like Twizzlers."

Out of the corner of my eye, I see this guy leaning forward over the bar, dousing his fries in vinegar, a wide grin practically splitting his face.

Is he serious?

Aidan's jaw twitches as he stares past me. There are only the four of us in here, but the silence is deafening.

"Finn," he grits out before mumbling, "Christ," under his breath. "Adelaide, I'm sorry. He thinks he's pretty slick, but—"

"Please don't hold this against me," I manage to say quietly before turning in my seat to look at this guy, Finn. "Twizzlers can leave some nasty whip marks, given the right velocity. Maybe you should watch yourself." Facing forward again, I push my glasses back up my nose and ask Aidan, "Are we ready to do this?"

Eyes wide, Aidan is working really hard to contain himself, but the older gentleman sitting at the bar barks out a deep belly laugh. Cheeks red above his full beard, he says something to the bartender in not English—maybe Irish? And the dude frowns and goes back to washing glasses or something.

"Sorry. Francie—he's the owner—just told Finn he's not going to be able to charm his way into your good graces. He thinks...well, I told you already." Aidan waves his hand and drinks down about a third of his beer. "What have we got then?" He scoots over and peers at my screen.

We work for a bit, and I think I'm getting a pretty good idea of what he wants for his site. It's all good until the air shifts, and I square my shoulders, the skin prickling along the back of my neck.

"Thought you might like a little warming up." Leaning heavily on the back of my chair, Finn refills my coffee cup. But he lingers, crowding me.

Don't react. He's just looking for a reaction.

And, when I think it's safe, I release the breath I'm holding.

He lets loose with another comment. "Personally, I think you're smoking hot. You've got me burning up."

He seriously thinks he's good at this.

I pull a strained breath in through my nose, hard enough to wiggle my septum ring I neatly tucked up—again, trying for that professional vibe. "You're burning up?"

"I am," he purrs. "Think you can help me?"

I twist my lips, assessing him. He's tall and lean. Just starting to put on some muscle. He looks like he's close to my age with an artfully tousled mop of dark-red curls. He's cute, but for the love of God...

"I'm not a doctor, but generally, antibiotics are a good idea to nip that shit in the bud. Some of those"—I dismissively flap my hand toward his pants—"diseases can be cleared up pretty quickly, from what I've heard."

2

"What's your sign?"

"Stop."

Finn

F rancie might be right. This girl is quick on the comebacks. And seriously witty. I like that.

"Should I sit and keep you company? Be your inspiration?" It looks like she's working on something for Aidan. I pull out the chair next to her, thinking I'll slide in close and keep working on her.

She looks at me over the top of her glasses and deadpans, "Or you could not."

"What's your name, love?"

"Don't you have work to tend to, Finn?" Aidan pipes up, giving me his annoyed big-brother look.

"Sure, yeah. They're knocking down the doors today. Clamoring for drinks with the storm going. Pretty shite move of you, making this lovely lady risk her safety out in this weather." I throw a wink her way. Girls cannot resist the Finn wink. Not in the least.

"Right, well, Francie just took the rubbish out to the bin, so you'd best look busy when he gets back, or he'll be on your arse."

I shoot Aidan a fuck-off look and take in the shades of deep, dark pink fading out to a delicate, light cotton-candy hue in her hair, which is all wound together on the top of her head. She looks like she's trying to hide behind her big sweater and wild hair, but there's no denying how cute she is. Fucking adorable really.

"Let me know if I can get you anything. I'm at your service..." I draw the last word out, hoping that she'll fill in her name for me.

Instead, she gives me a side-eye and goes back to her laptop. Fingers flying across the keys, her tongue resting against her top teeth. Not biting it, but kind of.

I need to up my game. Pour on the charm—the lucky charms—and see if I can get a taste of her. "Can I get you—"

The slamming of the back door cuts me off, mid pickup.

"Christ, Finn. Go move your car, and park it straight. Have you lost all your spatial awareness?" Francie bellows as he bursts through the door from the kitchen. "You'll be lucky to make it through the winter without your car getting hit again."

I roll my eyes and slide behind the bar to grab my keys. Aidan barks his obnoxious laugh and looks from the pink-haired pixie to me and back again, not even trying to hold his laughter back at all now.

"What?" I pause, pulling my jacket on. "What're you laughing at?" I scowl at Aidan sitting smugly with the girl I want to be chatting up.

"I just said it was kind of disappointing that someone so suave couldn't seem to get it in the right place on the first try," she replies. This girl keeps an absolutely solid dead stare while Aidan is laughing so hard, I think he might fall out of his chair. Actually, I hope the arse does.

"You don't need to worry about me sliding into tight spots. I can maneuver just fine."

Francie scoffs and shakes his head at me, pointing to the back door.

"I avoided a collision just today as I turned into the car park." Having made my point that I am in fact a stellar driver, I hustle out to straighten my car at the back of the building.

It takes me three tries to park my little Kia perfectly straight and even within the lines. I should probably get my eyes checked and see if I need a new prescription for my glasses. Maybe I'll get contact lenses this time. Though I've always heard that girls like a nerdy-looking guy, and I try hard to be everything the ladies could possibly want.

I wonder how long she's going to be here, working with Aidan. Maybe I should clean the snow off her car. Maybe she'll tell me her name if I do. It's not like there's anyone inside, waiting on me to serve them. It's just been the four of us since we opened, and I don't see the evening filling up too much.

When her car is cleaned off, I knock the snow from my boots at the back door and shake the flakes from my jacket before returning to the bar. My glasses are completely fogged up from the sudden change in temperature. I slide them off to clean them and I'm caught off guard by the finger in my chest.

"You're the asshole who swerved out front? You almost hit me!" She really is quite little, her head just clearing my shoulder.

"What are you on about?" I slide my glasses back on, so I can focus on her adorably annoyed expression.

"That car you almost hit this morning? That was me, asshole."

Her royal-blue fingernail jabs repeatedly into the center of my chest. And it hurts.

I grab her hand and bring her knuckles up to my lips, kissing them. "See then, we were destined to meet today," I croon at her. I totally have this thing in the bag. There's no way she can resist me.

My attention is drawn to the front door where Aidan is coming back in from outside. I don't see it coming, not at all. But, when she yanks her hand from mine and shoves her shoulder into my sternum, it knocks the wind from me.

She's a hell of a lot stronger than I gave her credit for.

"Your car's all cleared off. Is there anything I can carry for you, Adelaide?"

The arse just took credit for my work. I cleared the snow off her car, me.

"Thanks, but no." She shrugs on her coat and wraps a

blue-and-teal scarf around her neck. And then she pulls bright-green mittens out of her pockets.

She is a riot of color that I can't seem to take my eyes off of. She's captivating.

And she's walking out of the pub.

I have to do something. I need more time with her. I need for her to realize she wants me, needs me, can't live without me. I don't like losing.

"Maybe I'll run into you again sometime," I toss out to her. I lean back against the bar, feet spread and thumbs hooked in the pockets of my jeans. That leaves my fingers dangling, framing my goods. This move always works, gets the focus where I want it. The ladies can't resist me when I point out what I've got to offer.

When she turns in the doorway, framed by the snow falling outside, I give her the smile and wink. Hope lights up her features. I wiggle my fingers a little to draw her attention to what I'm sure she's thinking of.

And, with her eyes never leaving my face, her lip twitches as she says, "All flirt and no follow-through."

My smile fades as she turns and walks out of the pub. I almost don't hear Aidan laughing at me through the sting of her words, my mind locking in on her brush-off.

THE PUB never does fill up. Probably has more to do with the fact that it's a Tuesday night in January than the bit of snow we've gotten. Unfortunately, that means I'm bored. Nothing to do but wipe down bottles, bullshit with the handful of regulars who never miss stopping in, and think about what comes next.

I should probably go back to university and try again for a degree. I pull up the college website on my phone and look at the offerings. Teaching, nursing, business, computers. I have a fair bit of money in the bank. That happens when you share rent and work all the time.

I love my job; I do. I get to sleep late, drink at work, and have constant access to lovely, willing women. But I can't *just* tend bar for the rest of my life. I don't know what Francie's plans are for McBride's, but he's not getting any younger. Maybe a business degree will give me some options. Maybe I can help Francie, show him I'm responsible and that I can take on more responsibilities here at the pub.

"Finn, my man, how's the single life treating you?"

Andy's a regular, and he has been giving me shite for as long as I can remember. I slide his usual down the bar to him before continuing to wipe down the liquor bottles.

"Yeah, I'm good." I spin a bottle of whiskey round in my palm before dropping it back down in the well and picking up the rum to run my bar rag over it.

"Tell me about your latest. I have to live vicariously through you."

He quickly drains his pint, and I take it straight from him to refill. Andy needs a beer on the house every now and again. His youngest has been poorly, and things are tough at home for him.

"Erm, no one new today, man. Not since Marlee last

weekend." I throw him a smirk as the words tumble out of my mouth.

Marlee was really damn appreciative of the time we spent in her bed, her kitchen, and after that thing in the shower.

Christ, that shower.

I follow through. I had all kinds of follow-through with Marlee, and her neighbors can vouch for it.

"Andy, can I ask you a question?" I lean my hands against the bar for a moment, arms spread wide.

He wipes the beer off his upper lip and nods. "Sure."

"I follow through with things, yeah? I-I don't leave you hanging and wanting for more?" I pull at the label of the vodka bottle resting in front of me in the well.

"Uh, you give me beer when I need it. Is that what you're looking for? Validation in your job, Finn?" Andy chuckles as he takes another draught of his beer.

Everyone treats me like a joke, and I'm not sure what that's all about. I work hard. I'm here on time for almost all of my shifts, certainly more often than not. Chat with the patrons and entertain the ladies. I'm good at what I do. Better at some things than others, and I sure as shite haven't had any complaints in a long time.

3

"What's the difference between you and a calendar?"
"A calendar has dates."

Adelaide

idan's website is about finished. I have a handful of questions that I have to ask him, but they're things we need to go through in person. Face-to-face, and I'm avoiding that at all costs. He has been really easy to work with, making changes and adjustments, but I just don't want to have to leave my cozy apartment.

It's been snowing on and off for the past week since I went to McBride's for our initial meeting.

Eric is snuggling with me hard today, burrowed into the blanket draped across my big, comfy chair. He sighs and starts snoring lightly as I run my fingers down his back. This should be reason enough to never leave my apartment. There is so much contentment right here. It would be inconsiderate to disturb his peace.

Just as I'm about to close my eyes and take a little nap, my phone pings with an email notification from an older client wanting to tweak things yet again on her site. It's like the thousandth time she's decided to change everything. Everything. This is one of those reasons I don't like having to deal with people.

Maybe I did actually fall asleep for a bit because, when I open my email, I have four unread messages. Three from the continuing education program I work with and one from Aidan.

I fire off a response to my pain-in-the-ass client and let her know what to expect for additional fees. Thank God I put a PITA clause in her contract, outlining incremental charges for all changes after the third round.

Aidan is checking in to see if there is anything further I need from him. His girlfriend is ridiculously lucky. He is such a nice guy—kind, thoughtful, always concerned that he's being a pain in the ass.

Hardly.

The last set of emails gets progressively more urgent. The instructor who was lined up to teach a course on basic computer use bailed at the last minute. And they know I can't say no to them. Their computer programs are heavily attended by the cutest little old ladies. They help me when I'm missing my grandma, and I can't seem to resist them.

The new class starts this afternoon, so I slide out from under Eric and drag myself to the bathroom to shower and do my thing. I take a few extra moments to twist my hair into a funky braid before swiping on a coat of mascara and a little tinted lip balm. Though they frown at my septum piercing, the older ladies seem to like my colorful hair, and with Valentine's Day approaching, they'll probably make a big fuss over my festive pinks.

I shuffle through the posted syllabus for the continuing ed class and update the slides I have from the last time I filled in for this course. After checking my pantry and finding it woefully lacking, I pack up my computer and press a kiss just behind Eric's ear.

I need to stop on the way to the community center and pick up some cookies from the bakery. My ladies will be bringing me homemade cookies for the remainder of these classes, but since they don't know yet that it's me teaching, I need to make sure to bring some goodies.

The parking spot right out in front of the bakery and coffee shop opens up just as I approach. I park carefully, being mindful of the never-ending snow as I turn in. The selections inside are nothing short of mouthwatering, but knowing my ladies as I do, I stick with the giant, chewy chocolate chip cookies and the biggest, darkest roast coffee they have. My nap wasn't nearly long enough to knock the cobwebs from me.

Glancing at my phone, I check the time and hurry back out to my car. As I settle the box of cookies on the front seat and straighten up to grab my coffee off the roof of the car, I see a little silver hatchback careen past me down Main Street. There's no mistaking the fact that I know that car. It almost hit me, running me off the road the last time I was over this way.

Peering down the road, I see the car turn into the parking lot of McBride's, the wheels skidding wildly, the back of the car swerving until the driver regains control. A tall form unfolds itself from the driver's seat, and there's no doubt in my mind that it's him—Finn.

Is he out to get me for real?

By the time I get to the community center, my coffee is half-gone, and I have just enough time to make copies of my handouts before the ladies start showing up. Several of them have taken this course before. With me or one of the other instructors. I think they use it more for a social hour, but between this and the knitting classes they teach, they have a place to be. A place to hang out with each other and spend time with their friends. Lord, even in my head, it feels like I'm commenting on wayward youth as opposed to members of the grandparents and great-grands clubs.

Loaded down with coffee, cookies, handouts, and my computer bag, I stumble into the computer lab and almost drop it all before I catch myself. Thankfully, the only thing I manage not to save is the stack of handouts. They slide out of my arms, seemingly in slow motion, and scatter across the floor.

"Well, shit," comes the sweet voice behind me. Louise looks at the mess before waddling over to me to wrap me in a warm, rose-scented hug. "I'm so glad we have you this go around, Adelaide. That other guy they have teaching sometimes doesn't let us have cookie and coffee time." She looks genuinely put out by that inconvenience.

Squatting down, I gather the papers into a neat pile, placing the slightly wrinkled ones on the bottom.

"I stopped by Sweet Treats and brought the first round. Sorry. If I'd known I had this session before today, I'd have baked them myself." I look up and smile as the others start filing through the door. "Afternoon, ladies."

"Adelaide, honey, why do you bother with all that paper? You know we're not going to take them, sweetie." Connie sets her big floral bag on the floor next to *her* computer and makes grabby hands at me until I stand and let her hug me.

I'm so not a hugger. Nope. I don't like people, and I don't like being touched, let alone hugged. But this is different. And not a one of these surrogate grandmas is going to take *no* for an answer.

I unpack my laptop and connect it to the projector in case there's actually someone new signed up for this session who plans on learning the basics of using a computer. The roster I have shows my usual suspects, but there could be a last-minute attendee.

"Are you going to pass those treats around, or are you going to make an old lady walk for her cookie?" Virginia asks from the desk right next to the door. She's perfectly capable of walking the twenty feet, but she likes to play the poor-me card every now and then.

Connie turns and calls her out, "Virginia, how's that tai chi class you teach twice a week going?"

"Fine."

"Then, get your wrinkly ass up, and get your own damn cookie. You make people bend and breathe, but you think you can't walk for a cookie?" Connie dishes shit like no one else. No one, except Virginia because that woman is the master shit-slinger.

My heart is happy with this crazy crew. I make my way around the room, offering up cookies before we get started to avoid any catfights. It's blatantly obvious that I was not listed as the instructor for this session. My usually early attendees are dribbling in the door right up until the published start time. I guarantee, they will be early from here on out.

"Should we start this thing?" I ask while approaching the front of the room.

"Lord, yes," Ellie responds. "I thought we were getting stuck with that stuffy Richard this time around. Did you switch with him, dear?" She's looking at me over the top of her glasses as she turns on her monitor.

The rest of this crew though is snickering, a few mumbling about how stuffy Dick is.

I tilt my head from side to side and consider how to respond. I believe in honesty above all else, but I hate drama and sure as shit can't acknowledge their twelve-year-old sense of humor. And there is nothing a bunch of little old ladies love more than drama.

"I think you might have scared poor *Richard* off."

Eight sets of magnified eyes pop up to stare right at me. Some are surprised, a few are a tad bit confused, but most of them show nothing but barely contained mirth.

Master manipulators, the lot of them.

4

"ARE YOU JAMAICAN? BECAUSE JAMAICAN ME HOT."
"ACTUALLY, I'M FINNISH—SO FINNISHED WITH THIS
CONVERSATION."

Finn

I'm late. But it's not like this is a real class anyway. Once I made the decision to go back to university, I went out and bought myself a new laptop. The spot-faced salesman promised me the graphics were worth the extra money, and since I'll be using it mostly for social media, mostly Tumblr, until I can get into classes this summer, it seemed like a fantastic rationalization.

Now, I just need to get the instructor of this little community class to go through the setup on this thing, and I'll be good to go. I had to beg Aidan to fill in for me this afternoon, but once my laptop is all set up, I'll drop out and have no need for anyone to cover my Tuesday and

Thursday shifts. Instead of having to squint at my tiny phone screen, I'll have a crystal-clear, high-def, fifteen-inch screen for my Tumblr time.

I check the room number against the confirmation email I got when registering. The instructor is listed as Richard Johnson, but the voice I hear going over the course outline does not belong to a man. I planned on a guy getting the importance of Tumblr in full HDMI, but I can work with this. Maybe I can even get some extra credit out of the experience.

"I know we have a system, but we need to accomplish something this time. Turn your computers on, and..." The sweet voice does not match the vision at the front of the room.

It's the girl from the pub, Aidan's computer girl. Instead of being twirled up on top of her head, her hair is twisted into a pink rainbow plait hanging over her shoulder.

This is fantastic. Fan-fucking-tastic.

The last row of seats to the left of the door is empty, so I saunter over, drop my ruck on the desk, and shed my jacket. My zipper is the only sound in the room. I open my ruck and pull my new toy from the bag. The outlet is inconveniently located on the floor under the desk. Down on my knees, I plug in the cord and take a moment to make the necessary adjustments in my jeans.

Had Richard shown up to teach this, there would be no adjustment. But this girl? This girl has me off my game once again. In fact, she's got me so in my head, I don't notice the red Converse that have settled next to my desk.

"What are you doing here?"

Startled, I hit my head on the underside of the desk and pray there's no chewing gum stuck in my hair. I crawl out from my hiding space and look up at this girl. "I thought I'd brush up on my skills." It's not lost on me that I am literally on my knees in front of her, and I want to beg for a date, a taste, her name.

She rolls her eyes like it's an Olympic event and turns to take her place at the front of the room. I slide into my chair and finish setting up my command center. Laptop, phone, "water" bottle. I push my ruck down to the end of the table and lift the lid of my computer before cracking open my beverage.

"Are you ready?"

I look around the room and notice that I am the only guy here. And that all the ladies, other than the pink-haired love of my hour, are over the age of seventy and could give my gran a run for her money. But they're not giving me that hostile vibe. They look like they're thinking. Scheming. Up to no good for certain.

"Ready and willing, love." I swear, I see one of the ladies dabbing at her cleavage with a napkin. They all have napkins, some with half-eaten chocolate chip cookies from the bakery on them. "Erm, did I miss the portion of class where treats were handed out?"

I feel like I'm back in McBride's with the way she's rolling her eyes, and the over-seventy crowd is laughing at me.

"If I give you a treat, will you sit nicely and stay quiet?"

"Adelaide," the cleavage-dabber chides, "that's no way to speak to the nice young man."

Right, I knew I'd heard Aidan call her by name in the pub. "Addie, I'll do whatever you want, if you ask nicely and give me a little something for the effort."

The collective gasp momentarily wipes the smile from my face. But I didn't say anything too bad, did I? Plus, at least half of them have to be hard of hearing, right?

"Adelaide. It's Adelaide," she says with some bite in her tone, her teeth grinding against each other. "And you obviously aren't getting any treats." She stops herself just shy of stomping her foot and flicking me on the nose.

What does she think I am, a naughty dog?

"A word, dear. Stick with her full name, and you'll do fine." The lady across the aisle reaches over and pats my arm. "What's your name, cutie?"

"Finn O'Meara, ma'am." I shake her hand and use the manners my mum hammered into me. "It's a pleasure to meet you."

"Call me Virginia. You're not a native either then? Our Adelaide is a transplant from the Midwest," she says while offering me a cookie from her stash.

"No, ma'am. From Dublin, but I've been here for a few years." I reach out to take the cookie from my new best friend but pull back when I hear an outrageously loud throat clearing from the front of the class.

"I thought not," Addie scolds.

I grin innocently over the top of my bottle. "I'd be happy to share, if that would make amends."

The nip of whiskey I have in my bottle warms me as it slides down my throat. Not that I'm doing hard drinking, just a bit to make the class more tolerable. I offer the bottle to Addie because, if I'm honest, the only lips in the room I'm interested in sharing space with are hers. Especially her plump lower lip. The one that she's abusing with her teeth. The one with just the tiniest smear of chocolate that she somehow misses with every nibble and bite. The one I've dreamed of having wrapped around my cock every night for the past week.

I throw her the Finn wink, hoping to distract her as I adjust my growing problem—again.

All I'm met with though is a mumbled, "Antibiotics," and a flip of her braid as she walks away.

5

"ARE THOSE SPACE PANTS? BECAUSE YOUR ASS IS OUT OF THIS WORLD!"
"NO, THESE ARE BASEBALL PANTS BECAUSE MY ASS IS OUT OF YOUR LEAGUE."

Adelaide

Finn's very presence is annoying the shit out of me. Why is he here? This is my place, my zone. These are some of the only people I actually like, and this is one of the few places I enjoy hanging out, outside of my cozy apartment. For the love of God, he's tainting it.

I do everything in my power to push him and his crazy, infuriating existence out of my mind. I'm here for my ladies. To fill my cup and get my grandma time in.

We go over the basics, just like I do at the start of every session. Turning on the computer, signing in, connecting to the internet. This is pretty much as far as we'll get today because the cookies are gone, and Esther is out of coffee. We all have our limits.

"Okay. So, we'll pick up here on Thursday. Does anyone need a handout?" I take the stacked papers and chuck them in the recycling bin.

"Erm, that's it? We're done for the day?" His feet are on the corner of the desk, and his crap is spread across all three workstations at the very back of the room.

"Do you really need to be here? Surely, you know how to check your email and Google shit." I shove his feet off the desktop and twist my lips to try to suppress my grin when he falls forward to catch himself.

"Adelaide, be nice to the young gentleman. He's a long way from his family, too," Virginia appeals for her new friend. Hers, not mine. "Maybe you'd like to be friends. Get a drink or a bite to eat after class."

Is she serious? Making playdates for me? Setting me up on a date with her grandson was one thing. This is entirely different. And not okay.

"We met last week and didn't hit it off, so…I'll pass."

"Surely, we can't be done. I've still not made it all the way through the setup, and—"

"What?"

"The laptop is new, and I thought…well, I thought you could help me get things set up, so I'll be ready to take classes in the next college session." He has the nerve to look around the room, silently pleading his case.

"You're ridiculous, you know that?" I just can't with him. "Go. You're perfectly capable of setting up and using your laptop. Why the hell did you get this one anyway?" I turn the machine, so I can see what the specs are and laugh. "Jesus Christ, you already have a shortcut on your desktop to—" I snap my head up, staring into his eyes, and clamp my lips tightly together.

Oh my God.

"Adelaide, are you okay? Your face looks like a tomato."

Lord have mercy, nothing gets by Connie, and she is closing in on me and the screen full of Tumblr GIFs.

I slam the top down and push the now-offending computer away from me. "This is not what we do here." I glance around the room before narrowing my eyes at him again. "If you plan on coming back on Thursday, you will be following the syllabus in an appropriate manner. Do you understand?" I used my stern voice. My I-mean-business voice. My do-not-even-fuck-with-me voice. And I expect him to be intimidated, embarrassed, something.

Instead, Finn stands up, so we're chest-to-chest—more like chest-to-stomach in my case—and he leans in to pick up his laptop.

"Oh, I plan on coming back, love. For every single class. I'll also be planning on that drink and the bite as well." He nods toward his new best friend and the class traitor. Taking a step back, he addresses the group as he slides all his miscellaneous crap into his bag, "Ladies, it's been a pleasure. As for you, Addie, I'll see you soon."

"It's Adelaide."

He slings his backpack over his shoulder and walks backward out of the room, waving as he goes.

"He's a cutie, isn't he?"

"And did you hear him with that accent?"

"And manners. With his, *Yes, ma'am*, it might just make an old lady swoon a little."

Not one of them is bothered by the shade I'm throwing their way. I pack up my computer and straighten the chairs, making my way to the door. My jaw is tight, and my head is down. I don't want to engage. I feel like they all turned on me a little.

A warm hand settles on my arm, startling me out of my thoughts. "Adelaide, you should give him a chance," Louise says softly.

I can't help but roll my eyes again at the idea of going out with Finn.

"Louise, he's just..." Sighing, I try to think of what I want to tell her. That he's a cheesy flirt? That the rumors I've heard are that he's a man-whore and more likely to have a flavor of the day as opposed to being the gentleman he's led them all to believe he is? And why do I care? I have Eric; he's all I need.

Louise wraps her arms around me and pulls me in tight. Maybe it's time for me to move back home. I miss my family, especially my grandma.

Squeezing her back and stuffing down my tears, I bark out an ugly laugh when she pats my back and says, "If nothing else, honey, get laid. You'll feel better."

6

"Your pants would look great on my bedroom floor."
"You can buy the same pair at Target for twenty dollars."

Finn

I should have probably gone back to my flat after that exchange with the fiery little thing, but I'm too keyed up. Instead, I stop in at McBride's for a pint and some food.

"You're done then? I'm away, home to Lis." Aidan claps a heavy hand down on my shoulder and plants a bar rag in the middle of my chest.

"Fuck's sake, you said you'd work for me tonight. I'm just in for a—"

"Sorry, Finn. Lis is home. She got done early and needs me."

"Christ, I can't catch a break anywhere today." I stow

my ruck under the bar and grab a glass for my pint, mumbling, "Just wanted to get my setup done, check out some GIFs, and take care of myself."

"What are you on about?" Aidan asks. "I thought you had your class today, yeah?"

I set the glass down to let the thick black beer settle and lean my ass against the bar. "I did. Didn't go to plan though."

Aidan huffs a laugh at me. "Turn out the instructor was a man?"

I hang my head and roll my shoulders. The last thing I want to do is let on that I'm hung up on—*haunted by*—his web designer. Aidan's such a protective arse; he'd probably never have her meet him here again if he knew. *What if they're done meeting up? What if his work with her is finished?*

"Finn, you all right? Need to talk something out?" He steps back up to the bar, concern written across his face.

"I'm fine," I mutter. "Just gonna drop some chips in the fryer before you leave, yeah? Give me a minute."

In the kitchen, I take a few moments to cool off in the walk-in freezer and try to collect myself. I should have just gone straight home. Addie has me off-balance and aching for her at the same time.

When I can't avoid it any longer, I grab a fresh bag of chips and drop a healthy—or rather, an unhealthy—portion into the fryer. I busy myself, cleaning the already-spotless kitchen while I wait for my food to cook. Aidan will be fine for a few extra minutes. And Lis won't be that upset with me for keeping him.

"You about done back here?" Aidan pops his head

through the door, eyebrows raised, pupils dancing. "Lis is waiting for me in—"

"Christ, man, don't rub it in. I'll be out in a second." I need to find someone to take my mind off matters. Or take them into my own hands.

"Let's go then. I don't want to keep her waiting." He smacks the doorjamb twice in quick succession and fixes me with a glare. The glare of a man about to go home to a beautiful woman. His beautiful woman.

Shaking my head, I drain and plate my chips with a liberal application of salt. I grab the vinegar and go back out front to the bar.

WHEN I SHOW up to the community center on Thursday afternoon, I'm prepared. I have water in my water bottle instead of whiskey and my own little snack pack of cookies, and I'm not entirely late. I've even hidden the shortcuts to Tumblr and Pornhub in a folder on my desktop titled *Homework*. Perfectly respectable.

My new friend, Virginia, nods and smiles to me as I take my seat across the aisle. Like a ripple effect, each row of ladies turns, smiles, and nods, murmuring their hellos until sweet Addie raises her head and fixes me with her gaze.

"You're back." Not a question, it's more of an annoyed observation.

"I am," I reply, smiling. "And I've brought my own

snack." I hold up my store-bought treat, feeling like I've got this thing handled.

Addie does the eye-roll thing again, and I have to admit, I'm a bit concerned for her. She seems to have a problem controlling that particular response. Like, I'm afraid she's going to strain herself.

Virginia though stands, grabs the bag of cookies out of my hand, and throws them in the rubbish bin. "We don't allow that shit in here, Finn. We have standards," she scolds.

My protest is on the tip of my tongue when she hands me a still-warm, gooey cookie from the plastic container on the desk in front of her.

Addie grumbles something about me not knowing standards if they smacked me upside the head, which isn't true at all. If I didn't have standards, I'd have gotten into more trouble in Dublin with my Humanities professor.

"Thank you, ma'am." I make an exaggerated show of manners that everyone seems to appreciate. Everyone, except Addie.

She turns back to her computer and prattles on about files and organizing them into folders.

I get a bit lost inside my head, listening to the gentle melody of her voice. She's lulling me into a trance with her soft, almost accentless tone. Well, she has no accent compared to most of the girls I chat up in the pub. They all seem to have that harsh edge that screams New York, whereas Addie is all rounded vowels and steady cadence.

Christ, she's stunning when she's focused on what she's doing. I'm so entranced, watching her, listening to her, that when I take a bite of the cookie Virginia so kindly bestowed upon me, I embarrass myself a little. The chocolate and sugary flavors explode in my mouth, causing my eyes to close and a groan to escape from low in my throat.

The room goes absolutely silent, and when I open my eyes, everyone's head is turned, and the cleavage-dabber is dabbing and fanning.

I drop my feet down from where I rested them on the desktop and swallow quickly. "This is spectacular." I hold up the remainder of the cookie and smile.

While the prevalent response is a murmured, "Oh, dear," the louder response, the one that makes its way to my waiting ears, is more of a, "You have got to be fucking kidding me."

"Are you done?" she asks more loudly, glaring at me across the room.

"I'd never finish before you," rolls off my tongue before I can think better of it. So, I wink at her. I wink hard and play it off like it's no big deal because, really, it's true. Despite what she threw at me in the pub, I flirt *and* follow through.

And the ladies? They're not nearly as hard of hearing as I hoped, as they are stifling their laughter while Addie's face turns the color of her hair.

7

"I was going to tell you a joke about my cock, but it was too long."
"Too bad because I was going to tell you one about my vagina, but you'll never get it."

Adelaide

I can't believe Finn just said that. I can't fucking believe it. I bite at my lip while my face flames red, and I try to compose myself. *Does he mean to say shit like that all the time? Does he not know how to tone it down?*

Putting forth my best effort to ignore the fool, I carry on with the rest of the material, sneaking an occasional glance Finn's way to make sure he's not doing anything inappropriate, like cruising Tumblr. Sadly, the only way I can even think of to check on that is to find his hands and maybe look for any exuberant adjustments.

Each time I glance up though, he's smirking at me,

hands in his lap, stroking his pen, but still. And, of course, he winks. Every. Dingle. Time. *Single*. I meant, every *single* time. Damn it. I just roll my eyes, unchecked, not giving a shit anymore if he notices.

I hang back as the room empties, hoping to avoid any more awkwardness. Finn holds the door and acts all valiant and chivalrous to the ladies. *My* ladies. I had them first, and now, I feel like I'm losing them to him. We haven't even been out on one date, and we're already having a custody battle. Wait, there will be *no* dates with the cheese-slinging Tumblr monkey. Nope.

Finally alone, I check my email and see that my Susie-change-a-lot client has yet another overhaul she wants me to do. My bank account gets fatter with every one of her whims, but she's starting to drive me insane.

Aidan responded to my meeting request, and thankfully, he's agreed to meet at the coffee shop. I pack my stuff up and notice that no one really said good-bye to me. Shoulders slumped, I grab my bag and head out the door, flipping off the lights as I go.

Finn is opening and closing car doors for Virginia and Louise. Maybe he is chivalrous. Maybe he misses his grandma, too. I don't know. But my heart breaks a little when I see Louise wrap him in a hug before she settles in her car.

With a deep breath, I tuck my head down against the wind and power-walk to my car. It's time for a change.

"THANK you so much for being flexible." Aidan assesses me as I settle at a table in the back corner of McBride's. "I have to cover for one of the bartenders for a bit and couldn't get away to the coffee shop. We shouldn't be bothered much over here." He's searching, trying to figure out what's different with me.

"It's green," I say, thinking that's all he needs, but he's still squinting his eyes and furrowing his brows. "My hair. It was time for a new color, so..." I just shrug. *Do I really want to share with him that I was feeling a little jealous, so I needed my hair to match? Probably not.* It sounds crazy enough when I think about it too hard, but I guess, if he pushes it, St. Patrick's Day would do for an excuse.

"Huh. It suits you, but so did the pink. I like it." He smiles as he brings me a fresh mug of coffee and a small pitcher of cream. "The website is fantastic, by the way." Aidan pulls a chair around next to me and places his glass of whiskey down on a coaster.

"Great. So, I just wanted to check with you on a couple of details before we launch it and optimize the search engines." I slide my finger across the touchpad, waking the screen, just as the door flies open.

Virginia, Louise, and Connie come tumbling in—with Finn.

They pass through the room to a table out of sight and settle into what looks like a conversation that's been going on for a while. I would like not to be sad, not to feel left out, but I do. They didn't even notice me. I wrap a lock of my mood-matching hair around my finger and try to ignore the cackles of laughter and blatant flirting across the room.

He's flirting with them. Like real flirting, gentle touches, eyes sparkling, genuine smiles. Not the cheesy shit he gives me.

"You all right, Adelaide?" Aidan's brows are pinched, concern written across his features.

"Um, yeah." I shake my head, clearing the errant thoughts away. "Let's get through this and get your new site launched."

Aidan looks back at the table full of whispers and laughter, pausing before turning back to me. "He's a good man. A little lost maybe but a good man."

My breath catches, and my spine stiffens. "Okay. What...what does that have to do with anything?" I ask. The edge in my voice is a little sharper than it needs to be.

"Not a thing. Just doing a good deed for the lad." He smirks at me before nodding at someone over my shoulder.

I assume it's the cheesy leprechaun, but I don't need to know.

"Well, charity is good for your Karma, I guess." The desire to finish this up and escape to home washes over me. I would love to call in sick to class tomorrow, but I know that'd just end up biting me in the ass. Hell, I'm the substitute. Who knows whom they'd call to fill in for me?

We make a few minor adjustments on his site and take care of finances, and then I'm done. Quickly and quietly, I wrap my scarf around my neck and grab my bag. I forego my jacket to escape just a little bit sooner.

"Okay, so thanks. Let me know if we need to tweak anything, make changes, whatever."

Aidan nods his thanks, and I bolt. I'm out.

Eric is surely waiting on me. At least he'll be excited to see me.

8

"YOUR BODY IS A TEMPLE."
"THERE ARE NO SERVICES TODAY."

Finn

I wasn't really sure what to think when the lovely ladies from class asked me to lunch on Monday, but I had the time free and figured I could pump them for some information on Addie. I never expected to see her in the pub with Aidan. I might have volunteered to work for Jimmy if I had known they were going to be meeting up here.

"I think you'd make a lovely couple." Virginia leans close, like she's sharing a secret.

"I don't think she's interested," I huff out. "She has a tendency to—"

"To cut you to the quick. I know," Louise cuts me off with a knowing nod. "Have you considered maybe a different approach?" She peers at me over the top of her reading glasses.

This conversation seems to have taken quite the turn.

Hell, I didn't even know I was looking for Addie to be interested. I thought I was just fixated on her since she seemed impervious to my obvious charms. I mean, I've tried all of my best moves. She just seems to dislike me more and more.

"Maybe bring a coffee to class for her tomorrow. And, of course, you'll want to work on your cookies." Connie grabs a pad of paper from her bag and starts writing a list or something.

"What do you mean, *my cookies*? Is that a euphemism for something?" I like getting a rise out of the girls, though I do need to know more about the cookie situation.

Connie passes me the top sheet of paper from her pad. "Here, just follow this exactly and bring them tomorrow with that coffee. Dark roast with—"

"A bit of cream, yeah." I look over Connie's recipe for chocolate-chocolate chunk cookies as I think about what I need to grab from the market on my way home.

The closing of the front door draws my attention away from my mental shopping list. Addie is gone, Aidan's getting the bar ready for the night, and all the girls are staring at me. I push my glasses back up my nose and run my hand through my hair as I look at each of them in turn.

"What?"

"Nothing, dear." Virginia pats my arm again and smiles at Louise and Connie. They're quite obviously plotting something.

They file out the door shortly after, talking about where to go for dinner. That adds to my confusion since it's only three o'clock in the afternoon.

"Who eats dinner this early?" I ask the empty table.

Aidan, of course, can't leave well enough alone. "Erm, your demographic is aging, yeah?"

I slouch back in my chair and throw him a glare over my shoulder. I wish I could just ask him for advice. Talk to him and be taken seriously for a change.

"Are you pouting then? Did they turn you down for lack of experience?"

Shoving back my chair, I stand and shrug into my jacket.

With my recipe safely in my pocket, I stalk toward the door before a gruff, "Oy," stops me in my tracks.

"What? Not done? Need to pile on more shite?" I'm a bit touchy, yeah, but I have reason to be. I take a lot of crap from Aidan and Francie.

"Not piling more on, just...she's lovely. Maybe you should tone it down and ask her out." Aidan sets a Guinness on the bar for himself and an extra, though there's no one else here just now.

I check the time on my phone and sigh. There's just enough time for a pint before the doctor's office closes. The market is right by my flat, so I should be able to get it all done tonight.

Shrugging my jacket back off, I settle at the bar. The cold pint gives me something to focus on for a bit while I compile my thoughts.

"You're concentrating on that awfully hard. What're

you thinking?" Aidan settles against the counter behind the bar and takes a pull from his own pint.

There's no way I'm going to tell him how his jab bothers me or why. Sure, I miss my brothers and would love for Aidan to fill that role, but there are some things I'm just not into sharing.

"When did you know with Lis? How did you know that she was worth taking out?"

"Worth taking out? If you're interested at all, take the chance. It might turn out to be nothing, not right for either of you. But it might turn into the best decision you've ever made. What's holding you back? I've not seen you leave with anyone in over a week."

My head snaps up to meet his inquisitive look. "I..." He's right. I think back to the last time I entertained one of my lovely friends. *Was it Marlee?* "I don't know why you're paying such close attention to my love life. Things on the rocks with you and Lissy again?"

Aidan levels me with a harsh glare, choosing to ignore my last statement. I set him to rights several months ago, and he's not above giving it back to me.

Christ, why have I been leaving the pub alone? It's not that I'm hurting for willing participants. My phone is full of numbers, and the pub is usually full of options.

"Finn, maybe it's time to stop fucking about. Get serious about something for a change."

"You marrying me off? I haven't even taken her out, for fuck's sake. What if we're not, erm...compatible?" *He's got to be kidding me.* "Just because you moved right in with Lis doesn't mean I'm on a similar schedule." Fucking lunacy is what this is. I push back from the bar and drain my Guinness. I've heard enough of his wisdom, and I grab my crap from the barstool next to me.

"Finn—"

"Nah, I'm done. I've things to do. Places to be."

The door slams behind me just after I throw him the finger over my shoulder. Aidan can fuck right off.

9

"They say some things just don't mix, but I think we have good enough chemistry to prove them wrong."
"I have no reaction to that."

Adelaide

"Did the instructor from the last class leave their coffee?"

There's an odd vibe in the room today. The ladies are looking far too innocent for real life.

"I don't believe so, dear."

Something is up for sure; Connie never calls me *dear*. And no one has opened the cookies.

"The coffee's for you. Just the way you take it," Finn casually throws out. He's here—not just on time, but early. And he's not wearing his glasses.

"Do you need to sit up here? Closer to the front, so you

can see?" *Maybe he forgot them. Maybe they're just another one of his cheesy props.*

He looks so different without the frames. I mean, he's good-looking regardless. I'm sure that helps his man-whore ways, but I can't seem to stop looking at him.

"I can see just fine, thanks. I went with contact lenses. Do you like the change?" He winks.

There is so much winking with him.

I'm getting a little lost in Finn's eyes. When he unfolds himself from his chair and stalks toward me, I force myself to look away. Aidan's words, his comments about Finn, run through my mind as he approaches. I pull my lower lip between my teeth when he stops in front of me and leans in close. I level him with my best side-eye. No way, no how is he going to make a move here. Not in front of the ladies.

Instead, he pops the lid off the cookie container, deftly flipping and catching it. The most amazing smell wafts out, enveloping me in chocolaty goodness. "I'll just pass these round the class before we get started then," he murmurs. And, like a gentleman, he takes the stack of napkins and makes his way through the room, stopping and chatting with each of the girls. Polite. Kind. Considerate.

This is not what I expected to see from him. I catch Virginia giving him a quick wink when she pats his hand. Seeing this side of him has me off-balance. It's so far from what I've come to expect. And, this time, when he saunters toward me, I'm biting at my lip for an entirely different reason.

"I think you'll find this a far better thing to chew on

than that lovely lip. Though I'd be happy to help with that if you need." He holds a cookie out to me.

"It's huge." I look up at him, not registering what I said until the cocky smile spreads across his face. Shaking my head, I prepare myself for the inevitable.

"It is—" Whatever he was going to say gets cut off by a loud throat clearing from over on Louise's side of the room. Finn snaps his mouth shut, nods, and goes back to his seat.

Flabbergasted. I'm completely flabbergasted.

I have no idea what's going on today. Turning back to my computer, I take a bite of Finn's cookie and moan.

A-fucking-mazing.

The buzz that started in the room goes completely silent. I chance a look over my shoulder and find all the ladies smirking. And Finn is staring at me, wide-eyed, shifting in his seat.

"I...'s really good," I mumble around the warm, gooey treat. "Sorry. Let's, um...should we..." I never get flustered like this. "Fuck." This can't get any worse. I need to get a grip.

I don't know how we make it to the end of our class time, but I'm pretty damn sure it's the least productive class I've ever led.

"So, we'll just pick up here next time."

And, with that, the awkward filing out of the room commences. The air has been charged for the entire hour and a half that we've been here. I pack up my stuff, eyeing the rest of my cookie. There's no way I could risk taking another bite with an audience.

Finn, however, hasn't moved from his seat.

"Did you make these?" I wave toward my half-eaten treat. His response is nothing more than a slow nod. "They're delicious."

"Thank you," he rasps, still not moving from his seat.

"Here." I shove the container holding the remaining cookies toward him.

He shakes his head, pulling his computer off the desk and settling it on his lap. "No, you take 'em." His accent is thicker, more pronounced than usual.

"Okay. Are you, um...are you ready to go?"

"Erm, I am." He nods, sliding his stuff into his bag, waiting for me to pass before coming to his feet. "Can I help you with your coat?" He takes it from my hand and holds it for me, guiding it up my arms and settling it on my shoulders.

"Thank you." I have to clear my throat to make the words come out. I gather the rest of my things from my desk and pop a stray crumb in my mouth. A moan bubbles up unbidden, and I try to stifle it by pressing my hand to my lips. "Sorry," I mumble, cheeks flaming.

Finn follows me out of the room, turning off the lights and closing the door behind us. He walks me to my car and gets the door for me—just like he did for the ladies.

"I guess I'll see you...later?" I don't know why that comes out as a question. I mean, I assume I'll just see him back here in a couple of days.

"Sure." He nods at me, tight-lipped, and closes my door.

Finn steps back, and as I pull out of the lot, he's still standing in that same spot. Bag slung over his shoulder, jacket clutched at his waist, shivering in the winter cold.

10

_____

"*YOUR PLACE OR MINE?*"
"*BOTH. YOU GO TO YOUR PLACE, AND I'LL GO TO MINE.*"

Finn

I hope to God she didn't notice my struggle, my discomfort. But Jesus, Mary, and Joseph, when she moaned around that cookie, my cock was paying attention and didn't seem to want to let the issue go. Instead, I sat there, imagining the sounds she'd make with my lips around her clit.

Christ, I wasn't sure I had it in me to behave like a gentleman and not slip back into the tried-and-true methods that have yet to fail me. Until now. She seems impervious to my usual charms.

Today was different though. She didn't just dismiss me like usual. Maybe Virginia is right about tempering my approach.

Addie's eyes didn't hold the same disdain that they had in the past. It was like she appreciated my manners. But, fuck me, when she made the *huge* comment, it took everything I had and a quick reminder from my cheer squad to bite my tongue.

Much as I would love to get a handle on my *situation*, I've traded a lot of shifts with Jimmy, and I need to go to the pub and work. And shake myself out of this slump I've been in.

Maybe Virginia was mistaken about Addie's interest, though. Aidan is off his tits in love and thinks everyone should fall in line with that. I probably just need to find a lovely someone to help ease my suffering, to take my mind off relationships.

NONE of them strike my fancy. Not a single one.

Not a second glance.

Not a twitch.

Nothing.

The only thing that interests me and might possibly occupy my thoughts is another whiskey. I've already drunk more than my share tonight. But, as I pour another measure into my glass, the door opens, and finally, there's a reason to smile.

"Hey. I, um..." She approaches the corner of the bar and nervously looks around. "I brought your container back." She sets the plastic box on the counter. Nods and turns toward the door.

"Stay for a bit, Addie. Can I get you a drink?"

Any progress I thought I was making with her disintegrates as her spine stiffens, and her shoulders rise until they're practically lost in the green tresses twisted up at the base of her neck.

"It's Adelaide." I can practically hear her molars grinding, but I follow her to the door, like a lamb being led to slaughter.

"What's wrong with ye, Addie?" Before I realize I've done it, my finger is wrapped up in a soft green tendril that's escaped from the rest. "I like this color. It suits you."

Her sneakers squeak against the cement floor as she spins. She pulls her head back, releasing her hair from my grasp. "It's just Adelaide. Nonnegotiable."

Her head is tilted back, so she can meet my eyes. And glare at me evidently. My eyes dance across her features, taking in her deep-brown eyes and the silver hoop pierced from one nostril to the other. She's so unique, so different from other girls.

"What? Did you hear me? Nonnegotiable."

"I heard you, Addie." I open the door of McBride's, taking my business outside. Stepping into her, I lean down; she's ridiculously short. "And everything's negotiable," I whisper across her mouth, letting the door swing closed behind us.

Since she doesn't pull back, I press a kiss to those delicious lips.

Christ, they're more perfect than I imagined. And, when I sweep my tongue against the seam, she opens for me.

The last thing I want is for her to come to her senses too soon and pull away, so I slide my hands round the sides of her neck. I tilt her head a bit, just enough for me to nip at that plump lower lip that has been haunting my dreams for the past week or so.

Her hands grasp my forearms, and for a moment, I fully expect her to push me off. But she clings to me instead. So, I deepen the kiss, diving in for more. Tasting her. Teasing her. Taking my breath away—and, hopefully, hers as well. There's a current, sparks, crackling beneath the surface of my skin, and I want nothing more than to take her home. I want to peel back her layers and lay her bare. My mind swirls around the things I want to do to her. For her. With her.

So, when she pulls back a little, breaking the kiss, I try to blink my lustful thoughts down.

"I…" Her fingers ghost across her kiss-swollen lips, quivering slightly. "I have to go."

"You could wait until I'm done and go with me." I pull her hand and press her fingertips to my lips. *Fuck's sake, what if she says yes?*

Her pupils are blown wide, but she shakes her head. "I can't. I have to go home. There's some—I just…I have to go." She takes a wobbly step backward before fumbling in her pocket for her keys. "I'm sorry. I…"

Having her flustered is such a change. I like this.

"Good night, Addie. Sweet dreams." I shove my hands into the pockets of my jeans, watching to make sure she gets in her car safe. Without even thinking, I throw her the Finn wink.

She'll be back.

AS I'M CLEANING up for the night, Marlee floats through the door and settles herself at the bar.

"Hey, Finny," she purrs, leaning over the bar and flashing me her tits. "You almost done here?"

I can practically feel her gaze raking up and down my body. And, for the first time ever, it doesn't have any effect.

I just don't care.

"Marlee." I toss her a smile but have no real desire to engage her more than that.

What's happened? Our time together was spectacular, fucking mind-blowing. A couple of weeks ago, I'd have been looking for a repeat performance—or several. I mean, our evening was great. I was phenomenal, and Marlee certainly had nothing to complain about —repeatedly.

"So, do you already have plans tonight?" Her arms are crossed on the bar top, and with the way she's leaning over, her tits being pushed up as high as they can go, there's no awkward eye contact.

"Erm, no." I could so easily take her home and lose myself in physical pleasure. Making her scream and leaving her with just enough energy to give me a quick blow job before making her come until she passes out. I could, but—

"Your place? Or mine?" She licks her lips while she

talks to my dick, her eyes not venturing higher than my belt.

Why? Why does this feel cheap? Why does that bother me now when it never has before? Maybe I'm broken. It's been weeks since I've indulged with someone. In fact, I'm almost positive that Marlee's the last girl I've spent time with like that.

I casually fist a bar rag in both hands in front of me, shielding my poor, uninterested cock from her inspection.

"I think I'm going to pass, yeah..." *Think, Finn.* I search through the files in my brain for a solid excuse. "I've a headache, just going home to sleep."

Marlee stares at me like I've lost my mind before she shrugs and turns, walking out the door.

Maybe I *have* lost my mind.

11

*"Is that a mirror in your pocket? I think I can see myself
in your pants."*
"I don't think we're anywhere near the same size."

Adelaide

The entire drive home is lost to me. I was there,
awake and aware but not. Completely on autopi-
lot. I've never needed a friend to help me sort
something out like this before. My friends here have
proven to be more than biased toward the Irish Casanova,
and since it's after eight at night, they're most likely in bed
already anyway.

That whole antisocial thing I have going on is totally
biting me in the ass. I could talk to Eric about it, but I need
more. Another girl's perspective.

Climbing the stairs to my apartment, I text my friend
Brielle, hoping she's not out with her fiancé, Brad. She's

one of the few girls I hung out with in high school. We were pretty tight even though she's a couple of years older than me.

Instead of pinging with a notification, my phone buzzes, and Bri's smiling face lights up the screen.

"Hey, am I interrupting anything? You didn't need to actually call me."

"Oh my gosh, Adelaide, no. How are you?"

Hearing her voice makes me kind of miss my friend in Kansas City. I was so eager to get away, spread my wings, and start fresh that I never thought twice about the things I would be without, true friendships being one of them.

"I'm okay. I didn't pull you away from Brad, did I?"

"No." She snorts. "We need time and a bottle of wine for that story, but that's over. No more Brad. What's going on? You sound...I don't know...thinky." There's nothing like a librarian making up words.

"I am *thinky*, I guess." I don't touch on the Brad issue, because I'm thrilled that asshole is out of the picture.

"Is it a guy? A one-night stand who wants more? Is Eric still the only man in your life?" She giggles at the notion of Eric.

I unlock my door, grab his leash from the end table, and go straight for his crate. His little sausage-shaped body wiggles excitedly.

"He's more than enough testosterone for me. Usually." I settle him in my arm and head back down the stairs to let him do his thing.

"So, it is about a guy. Spill it."

I sigh heavily, thinking maybe I should have just slept

on the whole thing and then ignored it with every fiber of my being.

"I don't need a guy. Relationships are a pain in the ass. As a general rule, I don't like people enough to want to spend large amounts of time with any of them. I'm just not wired that way. I don't *people*."

"But?"

"But this guy has me all confused and rattled. I don't know, Bri. It makes no sense."

"What doesn't make sense, Adelaide?"

"He tends bar, and I thought he was nothing but bad pickup lines and one-night stands. Thinks his shit doesn't stink, and he's God's gift to women. I can't stand that shit." I scoop Eric up since he's done with his business and his short, little legs aren't conducive to two flights of stairs.

"Keep going. There's more you're not telling me."

"He's in my class—one that I'm teaching at the community center. And he's so sweet with my ladies. And he kissed me tonight. And, Bri, I thought I was going to die—like, my skin was all tight and tingly."

"Adelaide, sweetie, did your toes curl?"

"They did. They so did. And he stole my breath. Brielle, I don't know what to do," I whine, pushing through my door.

Eric scampers off to find his squeaky toy.

"Go out with him, Addie," she says softly. "Give him a chance. And, if nothing else, get laid. You'll feel better."

Letting the Addie thing slide because it's Bri, I snort-laugh at her advice. "That's exactly what Louise said."

"Well, listen to your elders. We've got experience on

you. Let me know how things go, okay? And, if all else fails, rub the nub."

"Okay, thanks. Maybe I'll come home soon. Catch up with you and the Brad sitch?"

"You know it. Night, babe." She hangs up before I can respond.

I throw myself back in my chair, hugging my knees to my chest. Not once since leaving Kansas City have I had a problem with a guy. Finding a release. Getting off and walking away.

It's not like I'm warm and fuzzy. I don't really like feeling—feelings. It's just sex, endorphins. And it's been a long fucking time. Since Eric came on the scene, the dachshund has been the only wiener in my apartment. Not even the guy who delivers my General Tso's chicken has stepped foot inside, and we see each other on the regular.

Pushing up out of the chair, I pad through my apartment to the fridge and grab a carton of leftover Chinese and a pair of chopsticks. The flavors bursting in my mouth elicit a small moan that makes me think back to class earlier.

To Finn.

To that kiss.

When he let go of his goofy, cheesy persona at McBride's and kissed me, more than my toes were affected. I felt that kiss race down my spine, expand through my skin, and set every part of me on fire.

It might have even sparked something in my soul. Thus, me off-balance. Feeling prickly and uncomfortable.

I can practically feel his warm hands grasping and

tilting my face, moving me where he wanted me. With our height difference, he could so easily overpower me, but it was nothing like that. He didn't try to take over in that moment; he just took control.

My God, if he's anything like that in bed...

Maybe I should listen to Brielle and Louise. Maybe they have a point. If nothing else, it could be some pretty amazing sex. And, really, I won't have to see him anymore after this class is done in a couple of weeks. This could work.

I finish eating and drop my bowl into the dishwasher. With all the thoughts of Finn's lips and the hint of getting laid, I'm definitely feeling twitchy. There's really only one thing to do, one thing that will afford me some relief.

Eric nips at my heels as I traipse down the hall to my bathroom. I fill the tub, testing the water temperature, adding cherry-and-vanilla-scented bath oil. Fragrance hangs in the heavy, humid air as I light a candle and slip out of my clothes. I hit the light switch and push Eric out, closing the door behind him. The last thing I need is a wiener ruining my moment.

With Eric safely out of my way, I sink low into the tub, steaming water caressing my curves. I slide my hand down my stomach and slip it between my thighs. Brielle's suggestion bounces around in my brain as my fingers tease and hint at the release my body needs.

As my climax builds, all I can think is, *What's Finn doing right now?*

12

"Looks like you dropped something
...my jaw."
"Looks like you dropped something, too
...your dignity."

Finn

The door slams behind me, interrupting the halfhearted moans coming from Jimmy's side of our flat. I stalk straight to the kitchen and grab a bottle of whiskey. Marlee's offer and my refusal sobered me far beyond where I want to end the night. I drain a fair bit of the bottle before resting it on the counter next to me.

"What's up your arse, Finn?" Jimmy walks out of his room in nothing but his boxers, slung low on his hips. He reeks of cheap perfume and sex.

"Nothin'." I rub at my eyes, not quite used to the contact lenses. I take another long pull from the bottle and wipe my mouth with the back of my hand. "Did I interrupt your big moment then?"

The whiskey is just taking the edge off whatever shite is running through my head.

"I got what I needed." He shrugs, reaching for the bottle.

I pull away, guarding it for myself. "You're a fucking selfish bastard, man."

"And you couldn't find a warm body to bring home, so you can fuck right off."

"Had the offer. Just wasn't the one I wanted," I boast, pushing off the counter and heading down the short hall toward my room. Green tresses swirl through my mind.

"You giving up the game?" Jimmy shouts after me.

"Just getting choosy," I toss back.

I strip down and warm the shower. The whiskey bottle gripped tightly in one hand, I step beneath the stream and tilt my head under the water. Surely, I can get some relief. My free hand slicks up and down the length of my cock, jerking, as thoughts of Addie fill my head. The way she tasted. The way she gripped my arms—not quite pulling me in, but not really pushing me away.

Christ, I've gotten my release any number of ways, but when I think of Addie, the feeling is entirely different. With my eyes squeezed shut, cock aching in my fist, my thoughts go straight to her. I wonder what she's doing at this God-given moment. The inkling that maybe, just maybe, she could be thinking of me has me stroking faster, harder.

I steady myself on the wall of the shower, whiskey

bottle clinking against the tiles. And the face I see when I come is Addie's, the look of pure lust when I took her lips earlier.

CHRIST, can I not wake up just once in the morning with my cock not aching for a change?

I close my eyes, hoping to fall back to sleep, but the ear-splitting wails of, "Jimmy, oh, Jimmy," are far too loud and not at all genuine, but they do the trick for me, killing any fantasy I might have fallen back into.

The man needs to pay attention to his girls' tells. Or have some fucking pride and find a girl who's a step further away from desperate.

I grab my earbuds and crank some music at a high enough volume to mask what I'd rather not experience. At least I take my time. Pay attention and leave whoever the lucky lady is satisfied but wishing for more.

WHEN I PUSH through the door of McBride's, only five minutes late for my shift, the last person I expect to see sitting at the bar is Francie. He's not been around much for the past few weeks, but with St. Patrick's Day quickly approaching, it makes sense that I'd be seeing a lot more of him.

"You're late again, Finn." Francie peers at me over the

top of his coffee mug. "What's your excuse's name this time?"

"Erm, Jimmy? That bastard is loud as fuck when he—"

"I don't need to know that." Francie holds his hand up, palm out, stopping my words. Hell, no one should be subjected to it. "What's goin' on wit' ye? I've heard that you've been keeping company with some *older* ladies again, not acting quite yourself."

"Been talking to Aidan then?"

I can take their shite and them riding my arse about things. I grew up with two older brothers who showed no mercy for taunting me until the day I left Dublin, but there are times I just wish the McBride's men would leave well enough alone.

"I have. Don't want you repeating history," he puts out there without any pretense. "He also mentioned a lovely little thing who is doing some work for him. I like her."

At that, I snap my head up to meet his inquisitive stare. "What did he say about her?"

"Finn, maybe it's time you settle yourself and take a break from the quick and easy."

My eyebrows disappear into my hairline at that.

He stands from the stool and pauses a moment, swaying a bit on his feet. "You're off this year for St. Paddy's. Why don't you ask her out? Take her someplace nice, treat her like a lady. And keep things respectful for a first date for a change." Francie nods at this sage advice and turns for his office.

13

"Do you have a map? Because I keep getting lost in your eyes."

"No, but you're right on track with getting lost."

Adelaide

I put off starting class, waiting to see if Finn will show. It's fifteen minutes after the hour, and he's not here. While I would've totally expected that the first week of class, I'm concerned now. He's been so punctual, early. And so involved with the ladies.

"Has anyone heard from Finn? Should we wait for him?" I flit my gaze from face to face and back to the door, searching for his now-familiar wide smile.

"He texted me that he's not feeling well, so he won't be here today," Virginia volunteers.

"You text?" The question falls out of my mouth, unbidden and completely without thought.

"Of course I do, Adelaide. I also tweet and snap." The look she gives me over the top of her glasses is nothing short of condescending.

"Is he okay? Does he need anything?" As soon as the questions tumble from my lips, I see the gears turning, and Virginia types furiously on her iPhone.

"He says not to worry; he'll manage. He'll maybe try to go to the market after a while if his fever's down." She reads from her screen. "I think it would be a nice gesture if one of us stopped by to check and see if he had everything he needed." She looks around the room, meeting every-one's eyes, before she blinks up at me. "Unfortunately, I've got to bounce after this, so..."

Virginia's declaration is followed up by a chorus of, "Oh, I wish I could," and, "I'm just not able to today."

"I would go, but I don't know where"—*ping*—"he lives." I glance down at my phone and see a text from Virginia with an address. When I look at her, her face is a mask of innocence.

"Might be nice if you brought him some soup or some-thing from the market, dear."

I should have paid closer attention.

AFTER FINISHING up at the community center, I swing through the market and pick up some homemade chicken noodle soup, crackers, and some ginger ale. And Twizzlers because, even when I'm feeling icky, it's nice to have a treat.

~

THE STREET that Virginia sent me to is full of cars with no parking spots in sight. As I turn the corner, I see a small lot behind the building and a spot open next to Finn's little silver Kia. Once I'm parked next to him, I grab the bags from the grocery store and climb the stairs.

I knock gingerly at the door. If he's feeling badly and sleeping, I don't want to be the ass who wakes him up. I shift my weight, popping one hip out and then the other as I wait. *Should I knock harder? Ring the bell?*

As I lift my hand to rap on the door one more time, it swings open, revealing some guy I've never seen before in my life.

"Oh. Sorry, I must have the wrong address." I back away, looking at the number on the mailbox and comparing it to the one Virginia sent.

"Not at all." The distinctly Irish accent washes over me. "You're looking for Finn then?" the dark-haired man says as he steps out of the apartment. "His is the room to the right, through the kitchen and down the hall a bit." He lopes down the stairs and disappears around the corner.

Tentatively, I step through the doorway and look around. It's every bit the bachelor pad. Worn dark-blue sofa, ridiculously large screen TV mounted on the wall with a gaming system sprawled on a makeshift shelf under it.

"Hello? Finn?"

It feels weird, walking through the space. Surely, the

guy who let me in would have texted Finn to let him know I was here. Well, that someone was here.

I pop into the kitchen and set the bags on the table in the corner. Busying myself, I empty the bags and consider digging through the cabinets for a bowl.

"Are you stalking me, sweet Addie?"

I almost drop the container of soup at the sound of Finn's raspy voice. When I turn, I'm faced with a lean, flushed chest and low-slung gray sweatpants, a roll of toilet paper trailing from his hand.

Damn it. What is it with stupid gray sweatpants?

"No. Virginia said you were sick, and I got *volun-told* to bring you soup and sick supplies." I narrow my eyes and point at him as he takes a step closer to me. "Keep your germs to yourself. I do not have time for sick shenanigans."

Finn's eyes are glassy, and his nose is red, like he's been wiping it with sandpaper. "Right. So, no kissing today." The words barely make it out before he sneezes three times back to back to back. "Fuck." He rips off a length of toilet paper and grimaces as he blows his nose.

I roll my eyes and replace the roll of TP with a box of super-soft, antiviral tissues. Then, I reach for the Lysol wipes I bought. Lord have mercy, germs are the devil. Snapping on the gloves I made sure to bring, I go on a mini-cleaning frenzy, wiping surfaces around the kitchen, throwing away trash, and straightening little bits of every-thing. I've gone completely into mom mode.

"I brought some chicken noodle soup. Which cabinet do you keep your bowls in?" I pull one down from where he's pointing and watch as a violent shiver rolls over him. "Finn, are you..."

He looks like he's burning up, goose bumps all over him, bright red painting his cheeks.

"Have you taken any medicine?"

"I haven't. 'M f-f-fine," he chatters, arms wrapped around his torso.

He's not. I shuffle him out to the couch and get him settled.

"Hang on, let me get you some Advil."

He's half-lying down when I come back with a glass of water, some pills, and the bowl of soup.

"Here, sit up for a minute." I hand him the water and pills, watching his grimace as he swallows. Replacing his water with the soup, I look around the room. "Do you have a blanket? Want me to get you a shirt or—"

"In my room, there's a quilt on my bed," he says as he starts in on the soup.

I don't know what I was expecting from his room, but the tidy, well thought-out space is not it. The soft cream-colored sheets, rumpled from sleep, are not the nasty dark ones that single guys usually go for. Like, since they're dark, they can get away with not washing them very often. His closet is open but organized. His shoes are lined up, clothes hung up neatly. It's just not what I imagined.

I pick up the handmade quilt pieced together in a mix of blues and grays. When I hug it to me, the fresh smell of fabric softener wafts up, and I inhale deeply.

"Did you find it?" Finn looks at me over the back of the

couch. "Christ, yes." He reaches back toward me, making grabby hands. "Are you sniffing my woobie?"

Eyes wide, I push it away from me and huff, "No. Did you finish your soup?"

I round the end of the couch, shaking out the quilt. Finn takes hold of it and pulls hard, sending me toppling to the cushion next to him.

"I did. Thank you." He stifles a yawn and settles into the corner of the couch. Broad shoulders, pale and lightly dusted with a smattering of freckles, slide out of sight as he wraps his blanket loosely around them. "You didn't bring me a pillow, too?"

"Would you like me to get you a pillow?" I ask, trying to force patience into my voice.

"I would." He tries to do his usual douchey smile, but cuddled with a blankie, his nose bright red and hair a tousled mess, he just looks freaking adorable.

"Fine," I sigh and grab a pillow from his bed. His very large, comfy-looking bed. I roll my eyes. The bed where he's taken countless women, if the rumors are correct. "Here." I chuck the pillow to him when he turns, and I start tidying up his tissues and bowl.

"Will you stay for a bit?" Finn calls as I scrub my hands under scalding water to kill any germs that might have gotten to me.

I dry my hands and bring him a fresh glass of water. He's completely snuggled in. Completely.

I shift from one foot to the other after setting his glass on the coffee table in front of him. "I don't know. I don't do germs well." Reaching up to center my septum ring, I panic for a beat, wondering if I washed my hands thoroughly enough.

"Please? Just till I fall asleep?" His eyes are drooping, so surely, it won't be long.

I slide onto the far end of the couch and suppress a shudder when he tucks his feet under my thigh. *What do I do?* I don't like feet any more than I like germs. Feet are disgusting unless they belong to an itty-bitty brand-new baby.

Oh my God. This is why I don't like people. They have germs. And feet.

Finn sleepily mumbles, "Thank you," as his eyes close and his breathing evens out.

I count to thirty, and then unclenching my fist, I tentatively reach out, touching his calf. The muscles are relaxed under my hand, so I push myself off the couch, trying not to disturb him. Finn rubs his feet together, the warmth of my ass no longer warming them. I pull at his quilt to cover him up better, but when I lift it, he shifts in his sleep, tucking one hand up under his pillow. And the other? The other is firmly in place, cupping his dick.

Of course.

14

"I KNOW HOW TO PLEASE A WOMAN."

"THEN, PLEASE...LEAVE ME ALONE."

Finn

I wake from what had to have been a dream. There's no way Addie would've been in my flat, tending to me while I was sick. But I'm wrapped in the quilt my mum made me while on the couch with a glass of water in front of me instead of whiskey. My quilt holds a subtle scent of something. Something soft and warm. Something I can't quite place, but it's familiar at the same time.

The distinct smell of disinfectant hangs in the air, and as I stumble into the kitchen, I take in the polished surfaces, the perfectly straight canisters, and a small stash of pain relievers and cold remedies. The fridge holds half a container of chicken soup and a full bottle of ginger ale. Things I know we did not have in the flat when I fell ill because I looked. I was fucking desperate for them. And the tissues are soft, soothing ones. Not the prickly roll of toilet paper I was using.

My smile stretches across my face as I read the note tucked under the meds. It's loopy girlie handwriting with the time marked for when I'm due my next dose. Christ, I slept like a baby. I shake out a few Advil and throw them back with ginger ale straight from the bottle. It wasn't a dream.

I shuffle to my bedroom, wrapped in my blanket, pillow tucked under my arm, and check my phone. No messages. No new contacts added. I dial the pub, and after no one answers, I text Jimmy.

Me: Did you buy food?

Jimmy: No.

Me: Did someone stop by? One of your…women?

Jimmy: Just the girl. Green hair, pierced nose, nice rack.

Me: You saw her rack?

Jimmy: She has great tits.

Me: I haven't seen them. How did you?

Jimmy: Relax. Used my imagination. She was being swallowed by a huge sweater thing. Nice legs though.

Me: Fuck right off. Did she leave a number?

Jimmy: No.

Me: Is Aidan there? Ask him for her number.

The bouncing dots taunt me while I straighten my bed and adjust the angle of the TV. I tilt the blinds so there's no glare on the screen, debating what to do next.

Jimmy: Sorry. He says no.

Why are they all against me? Because, now, I don't have her number, and all I can think of are her tits. Or the possibility of them since she always seems to be hiding under big, bulky jumpers.

Since Francie won't let me back to work yet, I watch movies, read, and think long and hard about what to do for myself—the next step in finding my place in the world. My purpose.

The application for university isn't difficult, but I hold my breath when I hit the request for my records from Dublin to be sent. That could ruin my chances. Francie and Aidan think I'm young and stupid now. I roll my eyes at the thought and can't help but think of Addie. Christ, she can roll her eyes gloriously. She thinks it's all tough and off-putting when she does it, but it just makes me wonder what she looks like when she loses herself in a moment of rapture.

Fuck, I've taken a lot of showers since she was here in my flat, and my cock has never been cleaner. I was sick, sure, but not sick enough to ignore the thought of her going into my room, into my space. If only I'd had her here and not been feverish. The mental image of her splayed out on my bed, green tresses spread out across my cream sheets, a hint of her perfume lingering. Her eyes rolling entirely from my efforts.

The frustration of not being able to break through her shell feeds the tedium of having nothing to do for the next few days. Add that to all of the anxiety from submitting my uni application and I can't seem to stop fidgeting. I glance

at my phone for the fiftieth time today, just as a text
pings in.

> **Virginia: How are you feeling, honey? Better?**
> **Me: Better. Bored though.**
> **Virginia: Did you have a visitor?**
> **Me: I did. I have no way to thank her. Can you
> help me?**

Why did I not think of this before? Of course Virginia has
Addie's phone number. Maybe I really am young and
stupid, but at least, now, I know what I'm doing in some
respects.

My phone pings again with a phone number from
Virginia. One not from this area code. I send a quick winky
face and enter the new number under Addie's name in my
Contacts.

Jimmy busts through the door, balancing a six-pack of
beer and a large pizza box. "Fucking lazy bastard. When ye
coming back to work?" He empties the contents of his
arms onto the coffee table and glares at me on the sofa.

The smell of Italian sausage and mushrooms wafts
through the room as I lift the lid of the box snagging a
piece. "I'm bored as fuck. Would love to get back to it," I
mumble around the huge bite of pizza.

Jimmy pops the top off a couple of bottles of beer and
hands me one. "Right. So, you'll take a few of my shifts this
week to make up for all your hours I worked?"

I owe him for certain, but I know what he's getting at.
And the answer is no.

"I'm not taking St. Patrick's Day. No."

"I've had to train the new kid all by myself," he whines. Legit whines, like a child. "Finn, you fucking owe me."

"Not that. I've not had a break on St. Paddy's in four years." I reach for another slice of pizza. "And my flute is feeling neglected," I deadpan.

Jimmy snorts beer out his nose.

I pop the pizza crust between my teeth and type out a quick text to the number Virginia sent me. My thumb hovers over the Send button, not quite ready to commit. I could call. Francie would tell me I should call instead of text. He'd tell me it was the proper way to say thank you.

But, if I call, she can opt not to answer and then just delete my voice mail. I'd never know if she listened or not. A text though? I can see that it's delivered and when it's read. With a text, I feel like I'll have a better grasp on her level of ignoring me. *What are the chances she didn't turn off those notifications?*

15

"IF THESE WALLS COULD TALK..."
"YOU'D PROBABLY MASTURBATE LESS."

Adelaide

Unknown: Thank you for coming by and taking
care of me.

Me: Who is this?

Unknown: How many sick people have you been
tending to?

Me: Finn? How did you get my number?

Unknown: It is. I wanted to thank you, and I didn't
want to wait for days to pass.

Me: You're welcome.

I slide my glasses to the top of my head and rub at my
eyes. This is about the last thing I expected. I've been
working nonstop for...glancing at the three-foot round
clock hanging high on my wall...six hours. I lost track of

time again, and now, I'm stiff. Hefting my computer and lap desk to the table next to the chair, I slowly start to unfold myself.

A low grumble of discontent sounds from under the blanket by my feet, and Eric wiggles his little body out, blinking at me. It's a standoff. If I hold perfectly still, he'll go back to sleep, but if I move an inch, there's no way I'll be able to put off his walk for even a minute. His eyes are just drifting closed when my phone vibrates with a handful of text messages back to back.

The sensation, while not at all unpleasant, startles the shit out of me since I dropped it in my lap after responding to Finn. It might have slid to strategically rest right against my lady bits. Eric takes my subtle shift as confirmation of his deepest desires, and he bolts for the door, sliding to a stop before he dances in an awkward circle.

Sighing, I push myself up, grab my jacket and bright-yellow scarf, and shove my feet into my boots. "Buddy, it's cold out. This is going to be a quickie," I tell Eric as I scoop him up to expedite the whole process.

Eric, of course, is oblivious to the cold and hops and skips down the sidewalk, looking for the ideal spot to poop. Honest to God, what makes the spot three blocks away from my warm apartment so much more desirable than the snow bank right outside the door? Dogs are stupid. Or maybe the male species in general are the stupid ones.

I'm frozen solid by the time we walk back through the door. Eric does his helicopter dance in front of his bowl for his post-poop feeding. So gross. I scoop out some kibble for him and go straight for my coffeemaker, fixing myself a fresh pot. The aroma fills the air around me as I fix myself a cup.

With my hands wrapped around the warm mug, I realize I have a big decision to make. *More work? Or lose myself in a book for an hour or two?* There's not really a question to it. I grab my Kindle, and after a few minutes, just when things are starting to heat up, the cushion under my ass shakes.

Shoving my hand down into the side of the chair, I dig around for a bit before scoring. There are a ton of text messages, almost as many emails, and a missed call. I don't talk to this many people in a given day, but there is someone new who has my number now.

"Eric, should I even look?"

Eric truly acts like he doesn't give a shit.

Swiping at the screen, I see that Brielle sent me a ton of pictures of her and Not Brad. The guy is seriously hot and looks super familiar, but I can't quite place why. The emails are from clients, and I decide to answer those later. The missed call is my dad. That's a no.

Nothing further from Finn. Another surprise. I figured he'd be all up in my business now that he had my number. He's not used to hearing no, and I have given him nothing but. I stare at my phone for a minute. Look around my apartment and take stock of my life. I'm twenty-five, I live alone, I work from home, and my best friend lives a thousand miles away and is sending me pictures of her and a hot guy who is definitely not her fiancé. My only consistent interaction is with a foot-long wiener named Eric.

And, now, I'm bothered that one of the man-whore bartenders has my number and is *not* blowing up my phone. I don't know what to do with this, but it doesn't look good for my social life.

I drop my Kindle and send a quick text to Bri, asking who the guy is, but the bouncy dots never bounce. Nothing. I pull a strand of hair from my braid and wrap it around my finger while I wait. The colors blend and shift as the strands wind and layer from deep, dark green to a much paler hue. I glance at my phone and still no bounce.

I'm lonely.

Really freaking lonely. It's never bothered me before. I like to be alone—like, really like it. No people. No germs. No feet. No attitude.

But it's lonely.

I check again, and there are still no bouncy dots. It's fine. My book will keep me company. I don't need anything else. I mean, I moved here to get away, so I'm away. I turn off notifications and drop my phone in my lap, diving back into my steamy story. But the silence is interrupted by a voice. Eric cocks his head from side to side, staring at my lap. At where my phone rests.

"Bri, is that you?" I call, fumbling with the button, so I can just put it on speaker. "Hang on, you're stuck between my thighs."

The laughter is deep, deeper than Brielle's voice. Maybe she's with that guy in her pictures. Lord, that would be mortifying. But, when I check my phone display, it's not my friend's number I see.

"I can't think of a better place to get stuck." The accent is raspy and a touch nasally, but it's his.

My fingers slide through my loose strands, and I groan. "Hey, Finn. I, uh...that wasn't meant for you."

"I'm not your Bri, but I wouldn't mind getting messages like that." He coughs out the last word and pulls the phone away from his mouth until he's back under control. "Sorry, that got away from me. Probably the excitement."

"You're not better yet? Do you need anything?" I guess I just assumed he was over this cold.

"Mostly better, no more fever, but—" He grunts a little, and it sounds like he's walking. "Sorry, I wanted some privacy. Since I've got you, erm...I, ehm..." He laughs quietly and blows out a barely audible, "Wow."

"You don't have me; let's just get that straight." Realizing how prickly that came out, I try to soften things. "But what do you need?"

"That didn't make it any easier to ask." Finn huffs out a laugh. "I would like to show you a good time."

"Show me a good time?" I snark. "You really think you're up for that?" *Does he even hear himself?* I gave him a chance. I tried to be nice. "Why don't you just—"

"That's not what I meant. I want to take you out," he rushes out. "Will you..." I hear a muted thud, like he banged his head against the wall or door or something. "Would you allow me to take you out on Friday evening?"

I'm stunned silent.

Whatever smart-ass direction I was about to tell him to go fuck off scatters from my brain when I hear a quiet, "Please."

"Okay."

"You will?"

I don't know what possessed me to say yes. Well, I do. It has everything to do with that whole lonely thing going on with me.

"Yeah. But I should go. I, um...I have to...I'll see you later."

"Bye, Addie."

"Adelaide. It's—"

And he's gone.

"Adelaide."

16

"I would go to the end of the world for you."
"Yes, but would you stay there?"

Finn

I don't know what to do.

I'm absolutely mental over this, where to take her, and Francie is not making things any easier. He keeps riding my arse about being a gentleman and not trying to get in her knickers on the first date. I've been trying to do that since I met her, and I don't know how to flip that on its head now.

Giving in to Jimmy's constant whining and begging for me to take his shift is starting to look like a good enough idea. I could tell her that I had to make up work from when I was sick, but that wouldn't be right. I don't think I can lie, nor do I really want to.

"Where are you taking your girl?" Francie asks.

"I don't know." I polish the very clean bar top.

"You have a date?" Aidan pulls the bottle of Jameson from under the taps and pours himself a substantial one.

"I do, but I..." I look around the pub. All the preparations for St. Patrick's Day are done. "Maybe I should cancel and help Jimmy and you." It makes sense really.

"*Pfft*, we've the new kid all trained up. Are ye nervous, Finn?" Francie, bless his heart, looks like he's worried for me.

I do feel a little off. Maybe I'm still sick.

"Who're you taking out that has you tied in knots?" Aidan looks from Francie to me and back again.

Jimmy picks this God-given moment to walk through the door. "Your Adelaide. Gonna loosen her up, yeah?"

"Christ, you're not." Aidan's eyes are wide, and his mouth is hanging open as he tries to make sense of what's happening. "Don't you fuck that up. She's a nice girl. You're not allowed to drive her away."

AND, because she wouldn't give me her address, we're meeting at McBride's.

On St. Patrick's Day.

With people packed in here and no room to fucking breathe.

Francie's at the door, checking IDs. Jimmy, Aidan, and the new kid, Kieran, are behind the bar, and I'm just standing here with my hands in my pockets, looking like a prat. The shattering of glass pulls my attention from the door, and Kieran's standing like a deer in headlights. He sputters an apology at Aidan, but when he leans down to pick up the bits of the bottle he dropped, Jimmy trips, sending the kid to his hands and knees. When Kieran sits back on his heels, there's a huge shard of glass sticking through his palm.

"Finn, can you..." Aidan nods toward the crowd of people filling the pub as he wraps Kieran's hand with a clean bar rag. He and Lis shuffle the kid out the door—taking him to the hospital, I'm sure.

I jump in and start pulling pitchers of beer and taking money, falling into the familiar rhythm of the past four years. Money. Beer. Whiskey. Flirt. As soon as I'm able, I reserve a spot at the bar for Addie, hoping she'll understand. *Hoping.*

I look up from another pitcher of green beer to see cascading emerald curls tumbling around the shoulders of an oversize cardigan. At least it's a million different shades of green. I set a mug of coffee in front of her, grabbing a carton of cream from the fridge.

"I'm so sorry," I start.

"It's okay. The guy at the door told me there was an emergency. Should we just forget this?"

I splash a bit of cream in her mug and tuck the carton away. "No." I'm leaning in, so I don't have to shout at her. "You look far too lovely and festive to waste this opportunity." I push the mug closer to her. "Do you mind waiting a bit? Maybe Aidan will come back." I get pulled back into the flurry of empty pitchers and waving dollar bills before she can answer.

It's an absolute madhouse, just as it is every year, and far too much time passes before I can take a breath and make my way back to Addie.

"Is this normal?" she shouts.

I grab her mug, refilling it as I knock a tap closed with my elbow.

"Pretty much. It's Francie's favorite day of the year." I nod toward the door and see the line is not going to let up anytime soon. "Usually, we have three of us back here, one at the door, and Francie keeping supplies stocked. We were a bit shorthanded to start and then..." I just shrug because more empty pitchers are being waved at me.

A few hours pass with Jimmy and me scrambling to keep up, and each spare moment is spent making sure Addie won't give up on me.

"Finn, baby, give me a beer and a shot!" a familiar voice yells.

I look up, and Marlee has her tits spilling out of a tiny green shirt. I do the best I can to make eye contact as I slide her a shot of whiskey and hand her a plastic cup of beer. Taking her money, I see a handful of guys behind her staring. Of course, she's wearing the shortest plaid skirt I think I've ever seen. And I've seen some short skirts over the years. The guys' jaws drop as she leans across the bar, grabbing my shirt to pull me in for a kiss.

Thankfully, Aidan and Lis breeze through the kitchen door just then, and I turn my head to greet them. And Marlee's lips land square on my cheek.

"I missed. Give me another chance, Finny."

Christ, she's off her tits already. I probably shouldn't have even served her.

I back away and nod at Aidan, wiping at the goopy, glossy mess on my cheek. "You back then? He's all right?" I look around for Kieran and only see Lis and her friend Gracyn.

"A bunch of stitches and some painkillers, so he'll not be back tonight. What was that?" Aidan nods at Marlee dancing her way over to the side of the bar. Right next to Addie.

"She's not taking no for an answer. I need to get out of here with Addie." I wipe my hands on a bar rag and hand it off to Aidan.

"Who?" He reaches out for an empty pitcher and falls into the repetitive motions of the night.

I glance to the right and smile as wide as I can—until I catch Marlee looking from me to Addie and back again.

I stalk over to them, smile firmly in place. "I'm done then. Let's get out of here, yeah?"

Unfortunately, Marlee is more than a little impaired.

"Sure, lemme jus' finish my beer," she slurs.

And the look Addie gives her is priceless—and more than a little intimidating.

"Heeeyyy, you don't have your glasses on. You look shexy like that."

Adelaide slides out of her barstool and makes her way through the crowd to the front door.

"I'll jus' sit right here." Marlee slides into the newly vacated seat, making herself at home.

"I'm out, Aidan. Maybe she just needs an Uber." I nod

toward Marlee as I grab my jacket from where I stowed it under the bar and push my way through to catch up with Addie. "You're not leaving, are you? Can I still take you for a bite?"

"Absolutely. I just hit my limit with people. Had to leave before Skankzilla got too close," she deadpans at me. "She always like that?"

"No. She's a hot mess tonight." I laugh as I guide Addie to my car.

She pauses when I open the door for her. "I've seen how you drive. Maybe we should take my car."

The way she bites her lip when she's being snarky does things to me. Things that make my jeans uncomfortable.

I manage to keep the car door between us to hide my growing erection. "I promise, you're in good hands. We'll be perfectly safe."

She climbs in, and I close the door, thankful to have the barrier while I make the necessary adjustments.

Unfortunately, with her seated, Addie's face is exactly level with my hand as I shift my cock.

17

"HAVEN'T I SEEN YOU SOMEWHERE BEFORE?"
"YES, THAT'S WHY I STOPPED GOING."

Adelaide

There is no denying that he's got something impressive there.

Finn clears his throat as he closes his car door and starts the car.

"Forget that was a window?" He pastes on his smirk and shifts his hips, opening his mouth for what I'm sure will be bullshit, but I cut him off, "Just be real for a change; no need to get cocky."

We both freeze. Neither one of us is willing to move a muscle until it can't be contained, and we bust out laughing.

"Cocky." When Finn repeats it, the snort-laughs start.

"Oh my God. Sorry, that was too funny." I swipe a

finger behind my glasses, dabbing at the tears. "What's the plan? What are we doing?" I shift in my seat to face him as he whips his car out of the space at the back of the lot.

"I had a plan, though it's all kind of gone to shite now with getting stuck at the pub for so long. Are you hungry? We could go get something to eat."

I've thought some horrible things about Finn and his driving. Who could blame me after he almost hit me and the way I've seen him zipping around town. But watching the way he handles the little hatchback, the confidence he has here, it not only matches how he moved in the chaos behind the bar, but it's also somehow better.

"I could eat." And I lose a little hold on my decorum as I watch him palm the stick shift, the way he grips it and strokes it like he's stroking himself.

He shifts in his seat and glances at me. I quickly look back up, hoping I didn't get caught staring, but—

"Whatcha looking at?" He quirks an eyebrow as he pulls into an impossibly tight parking spot at a restaurant.

"Nothing," I huff out.

He parked so that I have more space on my side of the car, so watching him slide his lean body out of his barely cracked door takes all of my attention. Hips flexing, ass tight, legs driving him up and out.

My hand clutches the door handle, knuckles going white as I grip it tightly. By the time Finn's around the car, opening my door, I have my breath under control, though my libido seems to be marching right along without a care in the world.

"You all right?" He puts his hand out to help me from the low seat.

Much as I need the help, I insist that I don't—because I'm not sure I can handle the contact—and almost wipe out as my feet hit a slippery spot on the ground. Finn catches me with a large hand firmly planted high on my waist, high enough that his thumb is almost grazing my boob. And the smug smile tells me he *knows* he's close.

"You sure you're okay?" he asks.

He's getting to me in more ways than he knows.

After the rocky start, we have a surprisingly normal dinner. My burger is perfectly pink and juicy, dripping in cheese, mushrooms sliding off the bun. My double-fried fries melt the mayo as I dip them.

"So, you came here for college and couldn't bear the thought of leaving?" Finn asks before licking some ranch off his thumb.

I'm wound so tight, everything he does makes me shift in my seat, seeking relief.

"Kind of. The program was great, and my scholarship was amazing, but I stayed"—I don't know how to say this without sounding like a petulant brat; maybe I am—"to win a passive-aggressive battle with my dad. He's a super-conservative lawyer, and he doesn't appreciate my style." I shrug, laughing a bit. "He'd rather I have golden highlights and clutch my pearls instead of my ever-changing hair and my pierced nose." I watch Finn for his reaction. We've hardly had a conversation, let alone a serious one touching on my less than conventional looks. "What about you?

Came for the women? Using the accent to its fullest potential?"

"Eh, no." He smiles, embarrassed. Maybe rueful. "I had an incident in Dublin and felt the need for a new start." He shoves a huge bite of his bacon cheeseburger in his mouth, darting his tongue along the seam of his lips.

I mentally shake the lust away, trying to focus on our conversation. *Conversation, good, Adelaide. Fucking him with your eyes, bad.*

"There's more to that story, Finn. You're going to have to tell me." That wasn't flirty at all, and the wink didn't really count. I might have potentially had dust in my eye. Or something.

"Ehm, well..." His blush comes hard and fast, but an answer doesn't.

Finn concentrates intensely on his fries, popping three into his mouth. Again with the licking of his fingers.

Why am I so focused on his mouth?

"I had an incident with my Humanities professor that ended poorly. My *married* Humanities professor." His smile is tight as he spins his pint glass back and forth on the table. "She kept her position, and I was asked to quietly leave university. My mum and dad told me to figure it out, so I did. I bought a plane ticket and came to visit my uncle in New York, and he hooked me up with a job." He shrugs and finally dances his eyes up to meet mine. And he's biting his damn lip.

"Wow, so...a married woman?" I stare at him, not quite sure what else to say.

"It was four years ago. I've learned a lot since then," he says earnestly.

There's an awkward pause, and then, with my eyes bugging out, I bust out laughing, my mind completely falling into the gutter. "I'm sure you have," I jeer.

"That is *not* what I meant." Finn laughs with me. "Christ, not what I meant at all."

We finish dinner and move on to discussions of Finn's seven siblings and the multitude of ways I've embarrassed my dad. Then, my work and his renewed thoughts of taking college classes.

Finn pays our bill and drives us back to my car at McBride's. He slides his car in next to mine. When he cuts the engine, his playlist continues softly with an amazing mix of indie and alternative rock.

"Thank you for sticking round and having dinner with me." He bites his lip and winks.

The wink has an entirely different effect than it used to. Or maybe I'm just really horny, but whatever. All I can think of is the way his lips feel and how sweet he's been.

Finn leans closer, tongue flicking across his bottom lip, drawing my gaze there. Again.

What starts out as a chaste, wholly appropriate good-night kiss is not nearly enough. The memory of our first kiss and all the lip-biting and finger-licking. The stick-shift-stroking, the cock-adjusting. I need more.

Unbuckling my seat belt, I plant my hand on the dashboard and push closer, deepening the kiss. But it's still not enough. I reach down between his legs and release the bar, sliding his seat all the way back.

Finn's eyes snap wide open, and a surprised smile stretches across his face. "Thanks for the ride."

I climb over the center console and settle on his thighs, straddling him. "Don't ruin this, Finn," I say against his lips, running my hands up his chest, grasping the zipper to open his jacket.

He pulls me closer, hands on my hips, grinding me on his very impressive cock.

Very impressive.

My elbow hits the steering wheel controls for the radio, raising the volume of the music, and the beat of the drum and thump of the bass fill the car. Finn pulls me against his chest, hands sliding up to push my cardigan down my arms. He leaves it wrapped around my wrists, trapping my hands behind me. There's no hiding my boobs like this, and the way he's staring is hungry and raw. He skims his hands up my waist, pausing high on my rib cage.

The anticipation is killing me. It's like he knows exactly where to touch me, how hard or light, to caress or squeeze. I lean in, ravenously kissing him, grinding down on him, fighting to free my hands. There's not nearly enough room in the front seat of this car, and in my struggle, I hit the steering wheel, blaring the horn.

"Christ, Addie. You're driving me mad." He pulls me tight against his cock, the pressure bringing me danger-ously close to orgasm.

The windows are fogged, the air in the car heavy with lust. I'm so close. So fucking close.

"Finn, 're you in there?" a very drunk female voice calls from outside the passenger side of his car.

We both freeze, panting and frustrated but trying to be completely still.

"D' you leave your car running, Finny?" The shadow of a palm is faintly outlined against the window by a street-lamp. "Finn?" Her singsonging his name is cut off by someone calling, "Marlee?"

Fingers trail away, a door slams, and the other car takes off, crunching gravel beneath the tires. It feels like we've been holding our breaths forever until it finally spills out in stuttered laughter.

"I guess I should go." I'm just as stuck, trying to get back into my sweater, as I was getting out of it.

Finn grasps the sides, sliding it up my arms, his knuckles resting against the swell of my boobs. "Maybe," he says gravelly. "Can I see you again though? I liked this —tonight."

"I'd like that."

He pulls me in for a sweet kiss before opening his door. He crawls out after me and makes his adjustments as we round the back of his car.

"Good night, Addie." Finn tucks me into my car with a final kiss.

I let it go, not correcting him this time.

18

"Sex with three people is a threesome. With two people, it's a twosome."

"Then, I know why they say you're handsome."

Finn

I sit in the parking lot of the pub for at least another half hour. The windows need to defog, and so does my brain. Or maybe I just need to get the blood flowing back in that direction.

I tilt my head back against the seat and close my eyes, willing my erection away. It's not an easy task when each time I think of Addie, I imagine the feel of her luscious tits in the palms of my hands. Jesus, I had no idea she had that body hiding beneath her loose T-shirts and oversize jumpers. Tight little arse, strong thighs, and that rack.

The drive home takes far too long, and the trek from my parking spot to the door feels like it takes even longer. I want nothing more than to sink into the memory of what Addie and I started in my car, but unfortunately, there's a ridiculously drunk girl passed out in the corner of my sofa.

Marlee's low-cut shirt is askew, and her skirt is doing very little to cover her arse. This is not the arse I was thinking about during the drive home.

I shake her, getting no response. Nothing.

Swearing, I drop my keys on the counter on the way to my room. I grab my quilt and a pillow. As soon as she feels the blanket on her, Marlee slides down on the couch, mumbling about steamed-up windows and breaking in. I grab a bottle of water and a bucket, setting it in front of her, just in case. This is not how I saw my night going.

After a quick text to Jimmy, explaining that there's an inebriated girl on the couch, I lock my bedroom door. I strip to my boxer briefs—the ones with the cartoon horseshoes all over them. I wore them for luck, and they worked perfectly—until Addie and I were interrupted.

My phone pings as I climb into bed.

Jimmy: Right. Couldn't make it to your room?

Me: Not Addie.

Jimmy: Fuck's sake?

Me: Marlee Ubered here. Picked the lock maybe and passed out.

I get a thumbs-up and nothing further. Jimmy's still got hours till closing and probably pitchers three bodies deep that need filling. If I were a better man, I'd have gone into the pub to help out instead of coming home straightaway, but I've been working there the longest out of all of us boys. I've earned my night off. And, with Addie on my mind, I'd have been useless anyway.

Christ, I'd probably scare the drunks with the ridiculous tent in my trousers. I'm concerned that the horseshoes on my briefs will forever be stretched out, never quite snapping back into shape. And there's no way I'll ever be able to sleep until I take matters in my own hands. So, I cue up my playlist from earlier—The UnBroken or maybe it was Of the Room—and reach deep for my much-needed release.

I WAKE in the morning to the sound of retching in the bathroom I just cleaned yesterday—you know, just in case. I should go help Marlee, bring her a glass of water, a spare toothbrush—something. But I don't. I lie in bed, waiting for the sounds of bad decisions to quiet, when it hits me. She fucking broke into my flat. Who does that?

Suddenly, I'm motivated to get dressed and talk to her, get to the meat of the matter. Find out what the fuck she was thinking. I pull on my jeans from last night and take a deep breath before stepping out into the flat.

"Marlee, you all right?" I ask, passing the bathroom, on my way to the kitchen. I grab a fresh bottle of water and take it back down the hall. "Marlee?"

The door swings open, and the wreck of a girl walks straight out, popping the bottle from my hand and wiping at her mouth. "Have you seen my phone?" She looks around the living room, shoving her hand down the side of the sofa and beneath the cushions. She plops down on her knees, her barely covered arse arched high in the air as she rests her head on the floor. "There it is." She stretches her arm flat under the sofa and retrieves her phone. Her dead phone. from the sneer and the hateful look she gives it.

"Can you give me a ride?" she asks. There's far too much suggestion in that simple question as her eyes rake down my bare chest, settling on the open button of my jeans. I really wish I had taken the time to throw a shirt on as well.

Fuck no.

"Erm, let me check my messages real quick." Hightailing it to my room, I grab my phone and shoot a text to Aidan, letting him know I'll take opening the pub today.

"Sorry, looks like I've got to fill in for Kieran, the new kid," I call out. Turning toward the door, I jump at the sight of Marlee propped against my doorjamb with her tiny T-shirt in her hand. "Ehm, here." I toss her my phone. "Call an Uber and go."

She catches the phone with a huff and scowls as she pulls up the app, tapping away at the screen.

"Just leave it on the kitchen counter, and lock the door behind you," I shout.

I'll have to ask her another time about how she got in here. Gathering my clean clothes, I head into the bathroom, making sure to lock the door behind me. It's a completely pointless act; if she broke into my flat, the lock on the bathroom door won't stop her.

I hold my breath and take the world's fastest shower, certainly the quickest I've ever done the morning after a first date. But, when I'm dried and dressed with contacts in, I'm thrilled to see my phone on the counter, the flat empty, and the front door locked.

PEOPLE SLOWLY TRICKLE in the day after.

St. Patrick's Day is Francie's favorite day, and while the tips are amazing that night, the day after is significantly less impressive.

Aidan texted me a very appreciative, *Thanks*, from both him and Lis.

Normally, my mind would head straight for the gutter, but he mentioned something the other day about a gallery showing or a photo shoot he had planned for this weekend. Between his talent and Addie's new website, his photography seems to be taking off.

I busy myself for the first couple of hours, stocking the beer cases, wiping down the bottles of liquor, and putting the tables to rights.

Francie ambles in mid-afternoon, box of doughnuts in hand, and settles himself at the bar with a cup of coffee. "I thought Aidan was taking the kid's morning shift," he grumbles, rubbing at his tired eyes.

"He's got some artsy shite to take care of, so I stepped in." I open the box from the bakery down the street and pluck out the chocolate-glazed doughnut, popping a big chunk into my mouth.

The look of surprise on his face makes me feel good and terrible at the same time. If a simple kindness shocks

Francie, then it might be time for me to make some changes.

"How was your evening with the girl?" He blows at the steam from his coffee.

"Lovely. She was absolutely lovely." The door opens, and my words get lost in my smile. It takes over my whole face; biting it back is fruitless.

"Well, and there she is," Francie announces, killing any doubt she might have had that we were talking about her. "Are you going to introduce me then, Finn?" he says, laughter dancing in his eyes. He can be such a prat when he wants to be.

"Addie, this is Francie." I gesture between them, adding, "And, Francie, this is Addie."

"Adelaide actually," she states.

I'm not thick. I catch it every single time she corrects me, but she's so bloody cute when she does it. Plus, I think she's starting to like it.

"Finn, get the lady a pint. Sit down, love, and tell me how your evening was."

Instead, I set a mug of coffee the way she likes it in front of her with a wink and smirk firmly in place.

"It was fine, good really."

My eyes are trained on her mouth as she takes a sip of coffee and then licks a drop off the rim of the mug.

Jesus, Mary, and Joseph, she's killing me.

I take a sip from my pint of Guinness as Francie asks, "And he was a gentleman? Kept his hands to himself, yeah?" The timing is unfortunate as I choke on a bit of foam, beer dribbling down my chin.

I'm stuck coughing, so I can't even respond.

Addie, thank God, has more grace in the moment. She assures him that I was perfectly well behaved. I grab the box of doughnuts and offer one to her before grabbing another for myself. Taking a bite, I hope the doughnuts are a distraction, and they get off this topic.

She chooses the other chocolate-glazed and moans around a sizeable bite. I must be staring. I'm honestly not quite sure that I'm breathing because I heard the start of that noise last night for an entirely different reason.

"Right. I'll just, erm...I have paperwork to do in the office," Francie states as he slides out of his seat, chuckling. "It was a pleasure, Adelaide." He nods and turns to face me, pinning me with all the fatherly warning he can cram into one look. "Finn."

That look speaks volumes. He knows something. Nothing specific, but I'm thinking he has a good idea that I was less than honorable.

I wait until I'm sure he's gone back before speaking. "Sorry about that. Francie can be a tad protective at times. He has a tendency to collect wayward youth and parent us."

I take another generous sip from my pint, and her lips quirk up on one side.

"Careful. You don't want to blow your load again."

How she can deliver lines with a straight face like that is fascinating. I, on the other hand, struggle to swallow my beer yet again.

Wiping the palm of my hand down my face, I collect

myself and answer with, "Maybe I do." I hit her with the wink that's almost automatic.

Addie looks away, dunking the doughnut in her coffee and giving me another moan.

"No, definitely, I do."

Her lips are wrapped around a delicate finger, licking the sticky glaze clean.

Surely, I'm developing brain damage, considering how often my blood seems to flow rapidly away from there. Closing my eyes, I count to ten and silently recite a Hail Mary before clearing my throat. "So, what brings you in today? I can't say this is normal, just stopping by."

"Hmm..." She pops her finger out of her mouth and tilts her head back and forth. "I wanted to see what your weekend looked like. See if you wanted to, um...watch a movie...or hang out?"

"Addie, are you asking if I want to Netflix and chill?"

19

"If there's a sock on my doorknob, don't come in. It means I'm having sex."
"Yeah, probably with the other one."

Adelaide

Finn ends up working all weekend, covering for the new guy. There's no way he can work with the twenty or so stitches in his hand and all the bandages.

Really, it's okay. I have my crazy client's website to completely redo. Again. So, I spend my weekend working on that, cleaning my apartment, and stroking my wiener. And reading.

But, when Finn has a lull at the bar, we text. All the texts. I've never really done this. It's a little like peopling but not. Flirting with a filter—I can handle that.

Late Monday afternoon, my phone pings and vibrates

while I'm hooking Eric up to his leash. My doxie is not big by any means, but he is a mighty little dick when properly motivated. He pulls and tugs his way down the sidewalk until he sniffs every tree, rock, and blade of grass, looking for the one that is magically just right.

I scramble to keep hold of the leash while checking my new message and trying not to drop my phone. Surprisingly, it's a lot to handle.

Finn: Are you still in your meeting?
Me: Nope.

The dots bounce for just a second, and then his number pops up with an incoming call. It's so weird to actually talk on the phone, and my skin feels itchy and tight as I hit the green button, answering, "Hey."

"Hi. How's your day? You met with a new client?"

"Yeah, someone Aidan referred. Um, it sounds like they want to work with me, so that's good." None of my calm and snark works on the phone. I feel put on the spot and stumble over my words.

"Excellent. Done enough of a deal to celebrate it?"

"Yeah. I thought—aren't you working tonight?"

"I plan on getting off and buying you breakfast," Finn responds. I can practically hear him wink with his comment.

"When and where should I meet you for food?" This is getting easier. I bite my lip and check to see if Eric is done yet.

"I might need a nap after, so eleven o'clock? And where depends on what you're up for."

"Who has good sausage?"

Finn's groan turns to a chuckle, and he mentions a diner not far from the community center.

"M'kay. I'll see you tomorrow," I say and end the call.

Kneeling down, I scoop Eric's tiny poop into a bright-green bag and chuck it in the nearest trash can. "Let's go, man."

BREAKFAST LASTS until well after noon with countless cups of coffee, a shared order of sausage, and ridiculous amounts of flirting. I really didn't even know I had it in me to flirt. Usually, I stick with prickly bitch. It works for me.

"Here." I pull some cash out to cover the bill.

"As if I'd let you pay for my sausage," Finn scoffs, shoving the money back at me. "You can have it for free."

I still roll my eyes at his cheesy comments but not quite as strenuously. I think there's more to him than he lets on, and it's kind of cute.

"Thank you." I slide out of the booth, and he places a hand at my back, guiding me out into the cloudy spring day. There's still a chill in the air, and a shiver runs through me.

"Are you cold?" Finn starts peeling his jacket off, but I wrap my black cardigan around me and smile.

"No, I'm good." I stop him. "I might just go to the coffee shop and work until it's time for class. It's warm there, and..." I shrug to heft my bag higher on my shoulder.

"They have tiramisu and coffee?" Finn adds, scooping said bag from my shoulder to his. He walks me to my SUV and settles me in the driver's seat. "I'll meet you there after I run by my flat. I just need to grab my laptop—unless you're going to share your Tumblr with me?" Winking, he leans across me, setting my bag on the passenger seat. Crowding me, pressing me into my seat.

"Yeah, no. I, uh, have to do actual work." His clean, citrusy scent surrounds me, invades my senses, as he slowly pulls his torso across me and smiles.

"Sorry, did I squish you? That was unintentional." He lingers a moment before closing the door with another wink.

Did he always wink this much? Is it his contact lenses bugging him? I kind of miss the nerdy glasses sometimes.

Lost in conversation, we walk into class together after spending the rest of the afternoon in comfortable silence, working at the coffee shop. Or at least, as silent as Finn could manage. The timing and our newfound amiability do not escape the ladies. Maybe it's the fact that Finn's hand is on my back as we walk through the door.

"Well, finally," Louise says as she pops open the top of her cookie container.

Setting my laptop and coffee on the desk, I scoff, "You know we don't have a designated snack time for this class, right?" When I look up, eight sets of owl eyes greet me.

"Oh, Adelaide. Not what we were referring to, dear." Virginia gives a side nod of her head toward Finn and waggles her eyebrows.

"You just make the cutest couple," Connie declares, followed by a chorus of, "Adorable," and, "Sweet," and other sentiments I usually bristle at. All the descriptors that my dad wanted me to embody back home. He wouldn't know what to do if he heard this crazy crew referring to me that way now. Like this.

My shoulders relax as I shake my head. "We went on one date. We're not a couple," I huff out, trying to blow them off a little.

My gaze is drawn to the back row where Finn is leaning his chair back on two legs with his hands clasped behind his head.

He smiles his cocky smile, replying, "Yet."

All of those owly eyes look back and forth between me and Finn.

"Shit. And, now, we're back to just a bunch of available old women in here, eating cookies. I signed up for a computer class, thinking I might meet a nice young man," one of our first-timers states.

"Really, Delores?" Connie asks. "All the nice young men know how to check their email already. You want to find nice young men, you have to go to the gym. Hell, even the hardware stores only have young moms doing DIY projects or grumpy old men trying to get away from nagging wives for an hour or so."

"It's true," Louise chimes in, plucking another cookie out of the box. "And is it even worth it at this stage? I'd rather just take care of *things* myself."

Oh sweet baby Jesus, no.

"Maybe we should talk about scanning and printing

documents?" I'd really like to avoid where I think this conversation is headed.

"*Maybe* what we should do is have one of those Love Nest parties," Connie suggests, looking around the room. "You know, like a Tupperware party but with vibrators?"

20

Adelaide

My apartment is by no means large. It works for Eric and me, and really, I don't have anyone else over. It's my space. Just for me. In fact, I don't think I've had anyone in since Eric was a puppy, and I had Chen set my takeout in the kitchen while I cleaned up an accident. That was months ago.

This is supposed to be casual, just our Netflix and chill, but after cleaning and straightening my living room three times, I decide I need a distraction. I dig through the pantry and find what I need.

The noodles are done, the four cheeses blended and melted into an amazingly smooth sauce. The bacon is crisp and crumbled. I assemble everything, unable to resist tasting as I go. With another heaping handful of cheese and the rest of the bacon on top, I slide the funky blue-and-green casserole dish into the oven.

Focused on getting things cleaned up before Finn arrives, I'm elbow-deep in suds. And he knocks. I grab a towel to dry my hands and hurry to the door, quietly opening it.

"Hey, come in. Quick." I tug on Finn's hand.

"Don't want the neighbors to get jealous?" he asks while leaning back into the hall, looking left and right.

"Oh my God, just get in here, and keep your voice down." The door finally closed, I pause with my finger on my lips and listen. Releasing my breath, I turn to Finn and smile.

"What was that about?"

And there it is. The thud of a body rolling off the bed, evidently taking my book and tablet with it.

"Is there someone else here? I thought you lived alone?" Finn looks totally disappointed.

"Yeah, brace yourself. That's Eric."

At that, Finn takes a step back and shoves his hands deep in his jeans pockets, disappointment turning abruptly to anger. His molars are grinding, his jaw twitching, cheeks flushing red.

"We've lived together for almost a year now." I can't contain my smile at Finn's scowl.

"Right." He nods and takes another step toward the door. He stops when I crouch down as the long reddish-brown body bolts down the hallway, skidding his back end out as he tries to navigate the corner.

I lift the doxie up and snuggle him into my side. "This is Eric."

Finn's jaw stops spasming, but his cheeks redden even more.

"Eric's a dog," he says, smile spreading slowly across his face.

"He is, and sometimes, he's a real dick, too. He tends to bolt out the door, and he thinks he needs to go as soon as he wakes up, so I was hoping to sneak you in, so he'd stay asleep for a while longer." I sigh, reaching for the leash. "Consistency is key with this guy, so I'll just—"

"I'll take him. It smells like you're cooking?" He inhales deeply and grins. "Let me tend to your wiener while you finish up." Scooping Eric out of my arms, Finn drops his voice, chuckling, "I'll slowly stroke him till we're out in public."

"CHRIST, THIS IS FUCKING AMAZING." Finn groans around a bite of mac and cheese. "Orgasmic."

It's good, I won't lie, but watching Finn enjoy it is so much better. "Do you want more?" I ask.

His tongue darts out, licking at the corner of his mouth. Swear to God, it does things to me.

Naughty things.

"I'd best hold back, so I don't explode."

My spoon clatters into the bowl at his words. Intentional or not, the double meaning zings through my core.

"Here, let me get that for you." Finn takes our dishes to

the kitchen, giving me a moment to calm my shit down. Not an easy task because the way those jeans hug his ass should be illegal.

"Do you have something queued up for the evening's entertainment?" he asks, coming back from the kitchen with fresh glasses of water for us.

"Guest's choice," I respond. "Sorry, I should have gotten some beer or something for you." I nod at the water glasses.

"This is fine. I can't claim that you got me drunk and took advantage of me." Finn grabs the remote and plops down in the middle of the couch, crowding me. Scrolling through the options, he finds a movie and starts it.

As he leans back into the sofa, he thrusts his hips up, sliding lower into the cushions before relaxing with a sigh. Shoulders melting, hand resting in his lap, legs falling open. He's completely comfortable while I'm wound so tight, I'm practically vibrating.

"The film is better than whatever it is you're looking at." He bites his lip, sliding his gaze to meet mine.

Suddenly warm, my cheeks flame, and I pull at my cardigan, settling it low around my arms. The air on my exposed shoulders does nothing to cool the fire burning through me as Finn traces my collarbone with his eyes.

"Maybe." I try, really try, to turn my attention to the show, but I have to fight the constant urge to look at him.

His hand slides over my thigh, coming to rest with his fingers tantalizingly close to my core. He stops progress and squeezes, digging his fingers into my muscles. I close my eyes, tensing even more.

"Then again…" he says, lips brushing softly against the side of my neck.

His tongue darts out, tasting my skin. Licking a trail down to my shoulder.

I tilt my head, granting him even better access. He sucks and licks and bites until he's pushed the strap of my tank top down to where my sweater sits, gathered at my elbow. His lips nudge at the lace of my bra. It's one of the few I have that can tame my boobs, and it happens to be the sexiest one I own. Turquoise, lacy, and makes the girls look fucking fantastic.

"I love this color. The pale of your skin peeking through the lace." Finn cups my breast, pushing it up, his thumb brushing over my hardened nipple. "The green tips of your braid splayed across it."

He closes his lips around my breast, sucking on my nipple through the lace. I arch my back, a soft moan tumbling from my lips.

Finn lavishes attention on one boob while tugging my tank top lower, revealing the other. "Christ, I'd never have guessed that you were hiding the most perfect tits." He licks deep into my cleavage—because, let's face it, there's *a lot* of depth there. "Fucking hell, Addie, you're gorgeous." He plants a kiss between the swells and meets my gaze. "And I mean more than just your magnificent tits."

Wrapping his fingers in the bulk of my sweater, he drags the material down, down, down, bunching it at my waist, my tank top going with it. I pull my arms free and run my fingers through his hair, grasping it in my fists. Pulling him into me.

"Oh my God, Finn."

His lips dance down the soft planes of my stomach, his arms wrapped around my hips, hands splayed across my back. We've shifted. Finn's body is covering mine. His chest resting between my thighs vibrates with a deep chuckle exactly where I need to feel him. My crazy-sensitive girl parts just fucking got a zing in the right direction.

Licking across the band of my leggings, Finn looks up at me, eyes hooded and full of lust. He grips the sides of my pants, fisting them in his warm hands. Waiting for my nod, my permission.

A breathy, "Yes," spills free, and Finn tugs, revealing the lacy boy shorts that match my bra.

Did I plan this? No. But I fucking hoped.

My tank top, leggings—all of it is stripped off and tossed to the floor. I lie on the couch with Finn sitting back on his knees between my legs. Fully clothed.

"You're a riot of color and beauty, Addie." He bites at his lip and palms the front of his jeans.

"You have far too many clothes on," I whisper.

"As do you," Finn replies as his finger dances down the lace of my panties, pausing and circling between my legs.

I slowly shake my head, pushing up onto my elbows. "Nope. Your turn." I clamp my thighs together to halt his hand but end up trapping it instead, between my thighs, driving myself more than a little insane.

With his free hand—the one not circling and kneading me—Finn reaches behind him and pulls his shirt off over his head.

Sliding his hand from between my thighs, Finn tosses

the shirt aside and lowers himself, pressing his lips to my clit, rubbing and licking through the lace. He pushes my thigh toward my chest, his thumb hooked around the side of my knee.

And his other hand? That one is working overtime, his jeans gaping open now, his hand gripping and sliding along his cock from root to tip and back again. I can barely see, but I know. I know what he's doing, getting us both where we need to be. Aroused and riled. Panting, thrusting, hearts racing.

"Finn. God, Finn—*uhngmagawd*—" I gasp as he pushes two fingers into me. Curling, stroking. His thumb circling my bundle of nerves. Never have I ever...*never*...

His name tumbles from my lips over and over, louder and louder. Until...until...

Fuuuuck...

"Addie..." Finn grunts, jerks, and stills just as my world explodes in lights and tremors and the most blissful release.

Ever.

21

"I could make you very happy."
"Why? Are you leaving?"

Finn

Never have I ever...

The way Addie came undone. The way she looked, wrapped up in that fucking turquoise lace. I never even got her completely naked. But I have never in my life seen sexier lingerie than Addie's. Doesn't even compare to the strappy scrap of black lace that books and movies seem so fond of.

And, as hard as we both came, that evening at her flat was...different for me. It changed something. Shifted it.

Made me think.

Consider.

She made me want the thing I hadn't allowed myself to even acknowledge since leaving Dublin. Jesus, fine. I'd considered it a million times but only in theory. Just the idea of it, not the reality. Not seeing it through. But, with Addie, things haven't followed my usual path in any way.

I have more time and energy invested in this thing— whatever it is—with her than with any other girl before, including my fucking Humanities professor.

Addie is a bundle of badass and pushback, but I can't imagine anyone I'd rather wrestle with.

And her dog, her little sausage. Eric and I bonded like men. Sure, I'd offered to walk him, but the little prick didn't seem to want to acquiesce and find a suitable place to piss. I had to encourage him, show him the way. We shared a moment behind the Chinese restaurant around the corner from her flat and marked the brick wall together.

Christ, and the way she moaned my name.

"Hey, love." I look up as she walks through the doors of the pub. "You're early. Kieran's not quite in."

His hand is finally healed enough for him to work again.

"Hey. How are you?" She's not shy with her affections, just shy around people in general.

I lean across the bar and push her boundaries a bit. "Give us a kiss, yeah?" I'm practically on my stomach, lying across the bar. But I get contact. Brushing my lips across hers, deepening it, savoring it.

"Remember when we had to kiss Finn for beer?"

"Yeah…it was only a year ago."

Lis and Gracyn are set up at the end of the bar, smiling at the interchange between Addie and me.

"You must be Adelaide. I'm Lis, Aidan's girlfriend"—sweet Lisbeth raises her whiskey glass toward Addie—"and this is my friend Gracyn."

"Hi. Yeah, I work for Aidan. With him really. Um, nice to meet you." Addie shifts her gaze from the girls to me, narrowing her eyes. "Do you kiss everyone? Like, all the time?"

Lis and Gracyn snort out a laugh, big grins and brows high. I don't mind them laughing at my shit near as much when Aidan and Francie do it.

Addie leans back, away from the bar, and snarks, "Damn, and I thought I was special."

"Oh, you are," Lis offers with Gracyn nodding in agreement.

"You've changed Finn—tamed the feral bartender."

I shake my head and finish stocking the beer cooler, leaving them to their conversation for a moment.

I guess I have changed. Sharing cookie recipes with the sassy seniors. Looking past all the enticing, willing women in the pub. I've kissed my share, pleasured more than a few. But the only one I think about now is Addie.

And she might have "tamed" me, but I've had some positive effect on her, too. Like tonight. We're going to see a band play live. If fucking Kieran ever shows up. He's late to every one of his shifts. Every single one. *Does he not consider his coworkers?*

Loaded down with a couple of cases of beer, I head back out front.

"Kansas City? There's a huge music festival there in the summer, right?" Gracyn's eyes are wide as she leans across Lis toward Addie.

"Yeah. The lineup is pretty amazing every year, but I think this year will be unreal. Did you know Lightning Strikes is from there? And so is Of the Room; I think they might be headlining."

Gracyn sits back in her seat, gnawing at her lip. She had a fling over her spring break last year with some guy in a band. I don't know details, it had a lasting effect on her, and not in a good way.

Kieran finally strolls through the door, tapping at his phone.

"Nice of you to grace us with your presence."

He nods his head, blond curls bouncing, not looking up from the screen, and mumbles, "Right," as he passes through to the kitchen.

"It's safe to leave him?" I look to Lis. "Does he even have a clue as to what he's doing?"

"That's part of why we're hanging out here. Francie asked us to 'check up on him,'" she whispers with air quotes in full effect.

"Jimmy trained him up, so..." I shrug. "When did *I* become the responsible one round here? Ladies, you're all right if we go then?"

Lis waves us off while Gracyn stares off into space, still lost in her thoughts.

"Adelaide, it was really nice to meet you finally." Lis smiles warmly.

"You, too." Addie waves as we push through the door.

"THAT WAS AMAZING. I kind of like your taste in music," Addie says as we leave the venue.

The show was fantastic. The lyrics raw, the bass and drums heavy, like I prefer. And the swaying hips of the gorgeous green-haired girl nearly killed me. More than once, I had to recite the rosary in Gaelic to keep from embarrassing myself.

"It was." I run a hand down the ocean that's her hair, my fingers lost in the waves. "Do you need to get home to Eric straightaway?" I open the car door for her, praying for her answer to be no.

Spinning so that she's facing me, wedged in the space between my body and the door, Addie runs her hands down my chest, curling her fingers around my belt. "Nope. He should be good for a while. Solid sleep when he's been properly exhausted."

Her breath is warm, and her lips are soft as I get the response I wanted, followed by a kiss to the hollow of my throat. She's gone far too quickly as she tucks herself into the car and winks at me.

I run around the back of the car, promising my cock the wait is done if all goes well. And, as short as the drive is back to my flat, it's considerably too long. The engine revs, and I jerk the stick shift from one gear to the next, abusing the transmission in a way I normally wouldn't.

Practically skidding into my parking space, I lean over, roughly kissing Addie before jumping from the car.

She meets me round the back and pushes me against the boot, pressing her little body into mine. "I really liked that band. They were...sexy, sultry." Her hands roam while mine pull her closer still.

I shove off the car, guiding her up the stairs to my door. "Keys are in my pocket," I mumble against the shell of her ear. Now that I've got her, I don't want to stop touching her for even a moment.

Her hands go to my jacket, finding them empty before sliding round to my arse and squeezing.

"Only one other place they could be." I think I'm being cheeky, but when she reaches in and slides her hand against the line of my cock, I suck a breath in through my teeth. *"Déan deifir.* They're right there." I resist the urge to grind my cock against her, knowing that's not going to get the keys in her hand any faster.

"What?" she gasps.

"Hurry up, love. We need to get this inside."

"Yeah, we do."

Keys finally in hand, I fumble with the lock, desperate to get inside.

We tumble through the door, grasping, kissing, nipping at one another. Lips and hands everywhere. Pushing and pulling at the layers of clothing separating us.

The timing couldn't be better. My mind was made up earlier that this would be it.

Addie's delicate, little hand cups my cock, squeezing slightly, and waves of lust and pleasure roll through me.

I spin us and pin her to the door when a voice breaks through the haze, a bucket of ice water to our sizzling passion. "Are you finally back, Finny?"

Addie's eyes go wide when she looks past me, but even that doesn't prepare me in any way for what I find. Marlee is on my fucking sofa, wearing nothing but knee socks, wrapped in my blue-and-gray quilt.

"Christ, Marlee. Not now."

Driving me back with a shove of her shoulder, Addie steps away from me. "Why is the drunk chick from McBride's naked on your couch, Finn?" Her glare is deadly.

"I let myself in, right, baby?" Marlee doesn't make any move to cover up, her tits on full display. Instead, she hoods her eyes, trailing a finger across her collarbone. "Just like St. Paddy's Day."

I cringe with everything I have.

"Oh, fuck no. Nope. No." Addie seethes, her green waves crashing with a vengeance around her shoulders.

I look between the women squaring off in my flat. This looks really bad. "Marlee, you need to leave."

"But you let me stay last time, Finny."

Sweet Mother of God, what is wrong with her?

"Yeah, I'll go. Leave you to have your fun with Bitchy McCuntface here." Addie shoves past and pulls the door so hard, it slams against the plasterboard, the handle denting it.

"Addie, wait."

She moves far faster than I would have ever guessed and is nearly to the cross street, tapping at her phone.

"Let me—"

"Nope. I don't have time for this shit, for your games. Go do your thing, Finn." She swipes at her cheek.

"That's not what this is." I reach for her arm as she slows to look for traffic.

She turns, her brows stretched high, and snorts out a laugh. Shaking off my hand, Addie spits out, "Obviously, I'm stupid, and you have your nights confused."

"Addie, I can explain," I plead.

A car pulls up to the curb across the street, and Addie rushes toward it.

"It's Adelaide." She slams the door of what I hope is an Uber, and she's gone.

Pissed off, I storm back to my flat and slam the door behind me. I hope to shit that Marlee is dressed and gone, but it turns out, I'm only half-right. Maybe more like twenty-five percent.

Pulling her long white-blonde hair out of the collar of her shirt, Marlee turns to me, smiling. "So, she's upset?" The simpering idiot pouts at me like she thinks she's being coy.

I drop my hands to my hips and start counting to ten.

Somewhere around seven, she laughs out. "But, damn, the green-haired chick is good with her bitch names." Marlee saunters across the room, stopping only when she's thoroughly invading my space. "I don't like to share, Finn. And I don't feel like I've been getting enough attention in this relationship." Her fingers curl into the waistband of my jeans, pulling me flush against her. Surgically-enhanced tits act as a barrier between us.

"Marlee"—I step back and remove her hand from where it sits far too close to my cock—"we hooked up, but that's it. One night. Not a relationship."

"But you ruined me. Finn," she purrs, sliding a hand up my chest, the other one gripping my completely uninterested knob, "I can't live without this in my life anymore. In my mouth, my p—"

"Stop. You'll live and find a sufficient replacement for your mouth." I put some serious distance between us, bending down to scoop up her tiny shorts.

But Marlee's forward, and her hands go straight for my arse. The contact propels me forward out of her reach once again.

Needing to keep some distance, I toss her the rest of her clothes. "Get dressed, and go, Marlee. No means no, and I'm not interested."

"But"—she pouts, stepping into her shorts—"you're the best I've ever had."

"You never actually had me, love. Now, tell me, how the fuck do you keep getting into my flat?"

"I borrowed my daddy's keys. He's your landlord." Marlee throws me a devious little smirk.

Fucking hell.

"Christ, are ye fuckin' kiddin' me?" My accent grows thicker with my anger.

"Not even a little. And you'll probably lose your security deposit." She runs her fingers over the dent from the door handle. "Unless you want to work out a trade."

"No." *Fuck no. No fucking way in hell.*

"What about your roommate?"

"Go." *What was I thinking when I took that one home? Oh, that's right. I wanted affection and looked for it anywhere I could get it, even with a scary skank like Marlee.*

"So, I'll just ask him directly." Her high, nasally giggle follows her out the door and down the stairs.

I need to warn Jimmy and start looking for a new place to live. But, first, I need to figure out a way to talk to Addie.

22

"What's it like, being the most beautiful girl in the pub?"
"What's it like, being the biggest liar in the world?"

Adelaide

F*urious.*

I don't talk to the Uber guy. There's no reason to bite his head off. I just seethe and cry angry fucking tears.

Irate.

Fucking incensed.

The words tumble through my mind as I search for the best one to describe this feeling. Sanskrit has ninety-six different words for love. The Eskimos have fifty. And I'm just sifting through all the words I can find for angry. There are some good ones, but none are quite strong enough.

Livid.

This whole thing can fuck right off.

I should have known, paid attention to the fact that he was nothing but a cheese-slinging Tumblr monkey. All about the lines. Picking up chicks. His conquests, scoring what he could, when he could and bragging all about it. Lowlife piece of shit.

The truly devastating part is that I did know. I'd heard all about the bar boys at McBride's when I was in college. I'd seen his flirting in class and in the pub and been on the receiving end of his cheese. And I still let myself be convinced that I was different.

Turns out, it doesn't matter how I set myself apart from whatever cookie-cutter mold there is, I'm just another chick. Apparently, there's nothing special here.

I don't know what to do with this feeling. I mean, I do.

Tears are still streaming down my face as I step out of the car and make my way up to my apartment. Fuming, raging, indignant tears.

I grab Eric from his crate and his leash from the table, and I head right back down the stairs. Consistency with this dog. Hooking the leash to his collar, I pause, letting a small laugh bubble its way past the tears. Every wiener should be properly restrained. The more I think about it, the more I giggle and snort. Thank God I have the sense of humor of a twelve-year-old boy.

I try to steer him to his usual patch of grass, but he tugs and pulls until he's found the perfect spot on the wall of the Chinese place. I probably have to find a new place to order my General Tso's since my dog is now peeing here.

And there it is. I have no control over the wieners in my world. None.

The rest of my night is filled with brownie batter. No need to waste time cooking that shit. It does the job just fine with a bowl and a spoon.

Eric burrows under the blankets and snuggles with me, doing everything he can to make me feel better, and after scrolling through my Pinterest board, I decide it's time for a change.

MY PHONE PINGS and vibrates during the next couple of days. Most of the calls and messages are from *Cúl Tóna*. I Googled how to say dickhead in Gaelic. Those go unanswered, and I don't bother even looking through the peephole when anyone knocks on the door. I'm not hiding. I just don't want to mess around with the Dick Who Shall Not Be Named.

I stepped out of my comfort zone and peopled, putting myself out there, and obviously, it didn't have great results. Not quite ready to deal with any of that, I throw myself into my real job.

Referrals have been flying in since I did Aidan's website, so many that I can easily lose myself in the quiet orderliness of designing and coding. All I need to do is get Eric's sleep cycle adjusted a little so that I don't have to leave my apartment as much during normal people times.

Eric, of course, is resistant to change. Most change since, all of a sudden, he can't seem to pass the damn

Chinese restaurant without having to pee on the wall. When there are treats involved, he's even quiet when the inevitable knocking starts on my door. Although the little dick does go cry at the door when he hears Finn's voice through it. There is nothing worse than a weepy wiener.

We'll get through this.

I work nonstop through the weekend and email the director at the community center, Anne, letting her know that I'm out for the rest of the classes. There are only a handful left, and to be honest, Virginia can cover them. She's taken that class so many times, she knows the material inside and out.

Anne isn't having it though.

"Adelaide, you're one of the best instructors we have. You're gifted with the ability to break down the concepts for the...more mature attendees," she quips.

I couldn't blow off her phone call.

"Maybe age is the problem," I mumble.

"Problem with what?"

"Nothing. Just thinking about a different problem."

"The young man currently enrolled in the class? Is he the one you're concerned with?" she asks softly.

"What? No—it's—he's—"

"Virginia called to let me know he won't be back. Was he inappropriate, honey? I've seen him around, usually helping the ladies into their cars, holding doors. Always using lovely manners, but then I'm sure age could be a factor there."

"He quit?"

"Mmhmm. Virginia didn't give a reason, just to let you

know. She said you'd most likely be calling to back out of
the rest of the session. So, since he's not an issue, we'll see
you tomorrow." Anne's singsong voice fades well before
she ends the call.

AND, true to that message, Finn's seat is empty. But they all
are. There is not a soul here today. My ladies are never late.
I glance around the room—from the door to the clock and
back again.

Finally, at five after, Louise walks in and hands me a
cup of coffee before sitting down.

"Thanks, Lou." I take a sip. "Where're the others?"

Before she can answer, Esther comes in with a box of
cookies. A small one just for me, and they look suspi-
ciously like the ones Finn made. She hands them to me
and hugs me.

Ellie walks through the door with a beautiful scarf tie-
dyed with pinks, teals, and blues. She wraps it around my
neck and plants a grandma kiss on my cheek. I'm stunned
absolutely silent.

Connie's next with a to-go container from the diner. I
crack open the lid even though I know what's in there. The
smell of sausage wafts out, and I snort-giggle, thinking of
how his cheesy comments started being kind of cute.

The gifts keep coming. A fresh box of the super-soft
tissues I brought him when he was sick. That one I open
right away to dab at the weird emotions leaking out of my
eyes.

"What is all this?" I sniff. Katherine just smiles and pats my arm.

No one responds. Instead, Sue walks in with a stuffed dog toy—Flounder from my favorite animated movie. She squeaks it twice before handing it to me and taking her seat.

Delores, the new student, walks through the door with a dog leash coiled in her hand. There are goofy sharks sporting oversize fins embroidered all down the length of it. Fins for Finn? I huff out a laugh, pursing my lips. I really want to just be pissed off, but he's making it really hard.

The ladies have dribbled in the door, bearing gifts, over the past half hour. Looking up, I'm met with seven sweet smiles. The only one missing is Virginia.

"He set you all up to do this?" I ask through some errant sniffles.

Not a peep. Normally, these women don't shush long enough for me to get through what I'm supposed to on a given day, but today, they have nothing to say.

Nothing.

Virginia slides up to the door and props her hip against it. "I like the new color." She nods at me, eyeing my blue-and-silver ombre waves.

"Thanks."

Virginia extends her arm, an envelope in her hand. "This is the last of it, honey. I'll take over class and keep the girls in line." She follows this up with a wink. A Finn wink.

I side-eye her pretty hard as I fumble to open the card without spilling my coffee. Surprised by the beautiful handwriting, I take in the words before looking up at Virginia. "Did you write this for him because—"

"Nope. My handwriting sucks, and you know it." She leans in and wraps me in a big hug, whispering, "Hear him out. That boy has it bad for you."

Connie hands me my computer case and a big floral bag full of all my presents.

Loaded down, I bite at my lip and reread his words as I stalk outside.

Adelaide,
> *Please come outside.*
> *—Finn*

"Why are you blocking my car, Finnegan?"

His car is angled behind mine, preventing my escape.

"It's just Finn. And I need to make sure you listen to me."

It's warm for the end of March. The sun is shining, and Finn has his sleeves rolled up past his elbows. He's leaning back, ass against the hood of his car, ankles crossed. Thumbs in his pockets, fingers dangling.

"What do I need to listen to, *Finnegan*? Stealing my best friends and having them do your dirty work isn't going to fix having BMCF naked on your couch." I pop my brows as high and judgy as I can manage, taking an exaggerated sip of my coffee.

"BMCF?"

"*Bitchy McCuntface.* Or has she been replaced with a new one since then?"

"No." He snorts out a laugh. "Well, yes, actually. And it's just Finn."

"We're done. Move your car, please, and let me leave, *Finnegan*."

He pushes off his car and walks toward me. Relieving me of my bags, he plucks my coffee from my hand and takes a sip before setting it on the roof of my SUV. "I won't. Not yet, not until you listen to me, Adelaide.

"Your BMCF, or Marlee, has been replaced. She was replaced a couple of months ago, about the time I tried to use a continuing ed class to get my new laptop set up. I met someone with a quick wit and a smart mouth, someone who's far more interesting." He takes a step closer to me, reaching out to slide a lock of hair through his fingers. "And it's just Finn. That's it, not short for anything."

"Fine, whatever. That doesn't change the fact that you were playing me. Having her spend the night after we went out? That's fucking shitty, *Finnegan*. And she has a key to your apartment?" I am full-on pissed, finger poking his chest, punctuating each word. "I was just the challenge. The chick who didn't buy your line of bullshit and give it up at the first flash of your cute fucking wink."

"You think my wink is cute?" He steps closer again, and his smile splits his face.

"Jesus, that's all you took from that?" Pushing against his chest, I try to give myself some space. Lord knows, I have to remind myself not to get lost in his eyes as it is.

"That was just my favorite part. But, no, I'm not toying with you. I did go home with her—once. Well before I met you. And, as for having access to my flat, her father is my landlord. She stole the key and let herself in. She was passed out drunk on St. Patrick's Day when I got home from our date. Christ, I had to sit in the fucking car park of McBride's for a half hour to let my windows clear and get some blood flow back to my brain. I was too exhausted to try to take her home, so I covered her up—on the sofa—and locked my bedroom door.

"And the other night? I don't know what that was. I've told her it can't happen again. Told her I'm not interested. At all." He takes the final step into my space, my back against the side of the car. "And, if you'd like, I'll call my mum. Right now, so we can settle the name thing." He slides his phone out of his pocket, taps at the screen, and holds it between us.

"What are you doing?"

The screen lights up with a video of a woman who can only be Finn's mother. They have the same dark-red curls, same cheekbones. The same mischievous grin.

"Mum, I need you to settle something for me."

"Of course, hon. Is that Addie with you? Hello, dear."

I try to blink away the fact that his mom knows who I am, but it's useless.

As I say, "Hello," Finn talks over me and says, "It's Adelaide, Mum. Anyway, what's my name? My full name."

He winks at me. That fucking wink kills me.

"Finn Francis Michael O'Meara. Have you hit your head and can't remember?" She winks the same damn wink.

"So, Finn's not short for anything?" His left eyebrow is

creeping higher up on his forehead as he waits for her answer.

"Of course not," Mrs. O'Meara scoffs. "What else can I help you with?"

"That's it, Mum. Thank you. I'll talk to you again at our regular time on Sunday, yeah?"

They blow kisses at each other and end the chat with a quick, "I love you."

"So, Adelaide, I am just Finn. And I never encouraged Marlee's behavior, and I hope to never encounter her again outside of McBride's. I'd be fine with never seeing her there again either. And I'd really like for us to pick up where we were so rudely interrupted." He tilts my face to meet his gaze.

He stares at my mouth as I chew at my bottom lip. I briefly look away before he draws my attention back to him, swiping his thumb over my poor, abused flesh.

I quickly rise up onto my toes, delivering a sweet kiss. "It's Addie."

23

"I DON'T WANT TO MAKE WAVES, BUT YOU COULD DEFINITELY
FLOAT MY BOAT."
"I AM FEELING A BIT WET."

Finn

I follow Addie back to her flat, sliding my car into a spot right next to hers. Jumping out, I grab her bags —all of them—from her car and sling them over my shoulder. I will proudly sport the big floral tote that Connie brought to get all the small gifts home in.

"You know, Eric is going to need attention before..." She trails off, and God love her, I hope she means...what I hope she means.

"I'll tend to your wiener while you put your prezzies away." I steal a kiss and snatch his new leash out of the bag.

"Oh, and I don't know what's up with him, but he's

been liking the Chinese place lately. He pees on the wall about halfway down the alley."

The dog and I share a look; he's a bit sheepish, but I'm nothing short of proud.

I scoop him up and run him down the stairs, outside and straight to the alley he seems to favor now. Of course, the little prick wants to take his time. Sniffing around, rooting under trash, generally drawing out the conclusion of his business.

"Be a good lad and go. Just get there, man."

But no...he's in and out of boxes, not even quick-like. He slowly drags his long snout along the top of each box as he slides back out, sometimes only to rush right back in and do it all over again, snuffling and panting as he goes.

Finally, when I'm about out of my mind, I swear, I hear him sigh. Having found what he was looking for, whatever that might be, he trots over to the wall and takes a long-drawn-out piss.

With his business done, I wrap my hands around Eric's girth, holding him tight and stroking him from tip to tail the whole way back to Addie's flat. When we burst through the door, he practically vibrates in my hands, and I release him with a bit of a grunt, relieved.

"Adelaide?" I almost can't breathe with my need to touch her. "Where are you?"

"Hey, right here," she replies from the doorway to her bedroom. "You okay? You're breathing kind of hard."

Her hair tumbles over her right shoulder, curling around her lush, gorgeous breast. The silvery blue is a stark contrast to her deep-purple T-shirt. A riot of color.

Closing the distance, I thread my fingers through her hair, thumbs tilting her head just so, and kiss the ever-loving fuck out of her. Not as sweet as I should be, not as reverent as I want to be. But heated, flaming passion spreads through every fiber of my being.

I pin her against the wall, unable to get close enough, needing to feel her against me. Addie slides her hands under my shirt, her palms cool against my blazing skin. I need more. Releasing her face, I kiss a trail down the side of her face until my nose is buried in the crook of her neck. I inhale her sweet, heady scent—a mixture of cherries and vanilla. She smells like dessert, good enough to eat.

I nip at the flesh where her neck gracefully meets her shoulder, soothing it with a kiss, and wrap my hands around the backs of her thighs. "Hold on," I rasp.

She gasps when I lift, clutching at my neck to steady herself, not that she needs to. I don't think I'll be letting her go anytime soon. I stalk through her room, not really looking where I'm going.

When my leg hits the side of the mattress, I plant a knee and set Addie in the middle of her soft bed. Not willing to let her go for even a moment, I cover her body with my own, forearms planted on either side of her. She's tiny, and now that I've got her here, I don't want to squish her. But, dear God, do I ever fucking want her.

Piece by piece, I peel off her layers. Her bright-yellow jumper, the black leggings she's got a preference for. Sitting back on my heels, Addie's thighs resting on my knees, I take a moment, allowing my gaze to wander over her pale, creamy skin and amazing fucking curves. I've certainly seen her in less, but with her splayed out on her bed—eyes bright and blue hair slashing color across the crisp white bedding—I want more than anything to see this through.

"I think," Addie draws out while hooking her feet under my arse, "you should get rid of some clothes, too." She curls up to sit and whips her T-shirt off, chucking it to the floor. She undoes the top few buttons of my shirt, trailing a delicate finger along my chest as she does.

I should move, rip my shirt off, but all I can do is stare. I'm not even sure I can breathe. Because, as Addie patiently undoes each button, I'm mesmerized by the vision in front of me. She's wrapped in creamy satin, a little navy bow nestled between her gorgeous tits. I'm definitely not breathing. In fact, I might pass out.

"Finn? *Finn?*"

I pull in a big lungful of air and try to focus.

"I thought I'd lost you for a minute."

"You did. You completely did."

Her hands are working at my belt, flipping open the button of my jeans, sliding the zip down. It's not until her delicate hands slide around my waist, pushing at the denim, that I snap out of my haze.

I twine my fingers through her hair, grasping a fistful, and pull her head back, exposing her neck to me. The swell of her breasts spills over the top of her bra. Kissing and nipping down that lovely valley, I push one strap down and then the next. As gorgeous as this is, I want it gone, out of my way. Addie reaches behind to release the hooks, freeing what have to be the world's most magnificent tits.

"*Fucking perfect*," I murmur against them. Stretching my fingers wide to try to contain them, not wanting to allow an inch of her skin to go unworshipped, I kiss and nibble from one to the other. Sucking and biting at her nipples. Drawing each one into my mouth and letting go with a pop.

Kicking out of my jeans and trainers, I push her back down into the pillows scattered across the top of her bed. "I want to taste every inch of you," I say, trailing my tongue down, down her flat stomach, teeth grazing and nipping at each of her hip bones.

The vanilla lotion on her skin tastes as good as it smells. She's fucking delicious.

I slide my hands beneath her hips, grab her navy-blue knickers, and pull at them until Addie lifts her hips.

She plants her feet on my hips, her toes nudging at my cock through my boxer briefs. "Finn?"

I close my eyes, taking a deep, controlling breath. "Addie?"

"Is that—"

"All for you, love."

"The four-leaf clovers on your undies?"

"Mmhmm. I wore them for luck." It takes all my concentration to keep my eyes from rolling to the back of my head. "You're going to want to stop doing that, love." I grab her ankles and push her feet to the side, sliding my palm up the length of her leg.

I wedge my shoulders between her thighs and lick her,

slow and lazy. Circling the tight, little bundle of nerves, sucking gently.

Today, this, with Addie will be an exercise in control. Patience. My feelings for this girl are so fucking overwhelming in every way. She has pushed me away, challenged my bullshit, and made me grovel and beg in a way I never have before. I've never been this invested. Not even back in Dublin when I thought I was surely in love. It never felt like this.

I slide one finger through her wetness and dip inside, pumping deliberately. Her moans, her gasps, the breathy sounds she makes drive me. I add a second finger and curl them, stroking and massaging that spot, the one that makes her gasp and shudder and sigh.

"Finn...oh dear God..." She tugs at my hair, not quite deciding whether to pull me closer or push me away. Her legs tremble and shake as she comes apart with my tongue on her clit and my name on her lips.

I leisurely kiss my way across her hips, up her stomach. Lavishing attention on her gorgeous tits, lifting them, feeling the heft of them resting in my palms. I bite her nipple, lightly tugging at her flesh. Addie reaches for me, drawing my lips to hers, tasting herself on me.

"You good?"

"So good. Do you have..." She lifts her hips, sliding her slickness against me. "Do you have a condom?"

Fuck, is this really happening?

"I—" *I can say no.* "I'm—"*I might be falling for you.* "I've —" I don't know how I'm capable of even the smallest thought.

"Top drawer on the left," she breathes against my neck.

I have one. I'm prepared, but the drawer is closer. I stretch across her body as she slides her hands into the waistband of my briefs, pushing them down my hips. I hand the foil packet to her and push back, freeing my cock and shoving the briefs away.

Addie rips the wrapper open, pulling the condom out.

Jesus, Mary, and Joseph.

The sight of her biting her lip, wanting me has me ready to explode.

I squeeze my cock and breathe deep, trying to find all the control I possibly can.

It's not a matter of wanting to. *Fuck's sake, I want this with her.*

My jaw muscles twitch as she reaches out, rolling the condom down my length. Nothing has ever felt as good as her fist on my cock. Nothing.

She squeezes lightly, and any thoughts I had of waiting, wondering are gone. All of them, gone.

Unable to keep my lips from her, I lean in, kissing her breathless. Or maybe I'm the breathless one. Addie shifts beneath me, sliding against me, nudging me closer...closer. She tilts her hips the last little fraction of an angle, and I'm right there.

Not moving.

Addie pulls back, searching my face, her gaze bouncing between my eyes. The connection is stronger than I could have ever imagined.

"You okay?"

"I am. Are you?" If nothing else, I have to make sure there's no doubt. None.

"God, yes."

She slides a foot up the back of my thigh, wrapping her legs around me. I inch forward, and a breathy moan escapes Addie as I slide the tip of my cock in. I thought her fist on my cock would send me to an early grave; I was mistaken.

In fact, nothing has ever felt as good as this.

"Addie, God help me...You're sure this is okay?"

"Yes, God, yes. Give it to me, Finn."

Her foot pushes against my arse until I'm there. Fully seated, bottomed out. Balls deep. Fucking surrounded by her in the most amazing way.

Every moment of intimacy before now were just lies wrapped up in a pretty little bow because sliding into Addie is the best feeling in the entire world.

Nothing has ever felt as good as this.

"Oh my God, Finn..."

I don't dare move a muscle. I don't fucking dare.

Gritting my teeth, I try desperately to run through the months of the year in Gaelic. Anything to keep control of myself.

"Holy Christ, woman. Fuck." *I think I might pass out.*

"You're not allowed to pass out, Finn. Let me...let me... please...*ohmagawd*..."

I thought I'd kept the passing out comment to myself, but I guess it slipped out. "Are you...are you okay? Sweet Jesus, please tell me I can move, Addie. I don't think I can hold still."

Before the words are out of my mouth, her hips start rocking, and I'm back to Gaelic. This time, I'm counting...

"*A haon, a dó...*"

Thrusting with each new number.

"Yes, Finn...more..."

Christ, her sounds are distracting in the best possible way.

"*A trí, a ceathair, fuisce, cíche...*"

Addie is meeting me thrust for thrust, and I'm fairly certain I've died and gone to heaven.

"*Ungmagawd*, Finn...Finn..."

Ah, fuck, God, she's amazing.

"*A cúig, a sé, glas, gorm...*" I reach between us and circle her clit, thrusting, counting, and saying random words in Gaelic. My spine tingles, and I know I don't have much time left.

"*Finn...*"

"*Tá tú álainn...*"

"*Please...*"

"*Ghlacann tú mo anáil ar shiúl...*"

Throwing her head back, Addie comes undone— again. Squeezing me, pulsing around my cock. When she opens her eyes, staring deep into my soul, I let go. My release ripping through me, like nothing I've ever experienced in my life.

Because until this moment, I haven't.

24

Adelaide

I run my nails down the center of his back, humming softly. "Finn, are you okay?" I laugh. "You didn't really pass out there, did you? Or die? Because that would really suck."

I can feel his chest expand and contract with each breath, but when he shakes with silent laughter, I don't fucking know what to think. Maybe it's relief or something.

"Addie, *is tú mo neamh*," he mumbles into the crook of my neck.

"What does that mean? You said a lot of things in there I didn't understand. It was almost like you were speaking in tongues." I smooth back his hair as he pushes up and smiles down at me.

"It was Gaelic. I said a lot of different things. I should, erm...get rid of this now, yeah?" Finn looks down to where we're still joined.

"The condom? Absolutely."

He grips the base and pulls out, both of us gasping a quiet, "Fuck," at the loss.

"Flush it then or..." He looks absolutely lost, like he's never done this before.

Surely, that's not right. Can't be.

"Knot it and trash?"

When he's back in bed, pulling the covers up over us, I settle half on top of him, chest-to-chest. "Can I ask you a question?"

He has a sweet, goofy smile plastered on his face, like he's all kinds of pleased with himself.

"You can, and then I'll tell you what I said in Gaelic." His gaze dances from my face to my boobs squished against his hard chest.

"Was that..." *How do I ask if this was his first time without offending him?* I feel like I should have known something like that beforehand. Plus, it's Finn, and he's known as one of the man-whores of McBride's, not that I really want to think about that. I'm no virgin, but...*holy shit.*

"My first time?"

I just stare at him, waiting.

"Was it terrible? Christ, I'm sorry, Addie." His whole body tenses, and he avoids meeting my eye. His jaw muscles twitch.

I place a palm on his cheek, drawing his attention to

me. "Not terrible at all," I tell him. "Truly, you blew my fucking mind, Finn. But..."

Finn snaps his eyes to me. "After what happened in Dublin, I just..." He licks his lips and looks deadly serious, shrugging. "I wasn't ready to actually go through with it. But it didn't completely suck?"

Oh, my heart. "We have a lot of things to discuss, but *that* did not suck at all. Not in the least." I place my hand on his belly and bite the lovely pectoral muscle that's right there, asking for it. "Now, tell me what happened in Dublin. Why did you have to leave school and the...Humanities?"

He nods, confirming that little nugget of knowledge.

"Why did she get to stay, and you had to leave?"

Finn flops his arm across his face, avoiding me as much as he can. "I mentioned she was, ehm, married, yeah?"

I nod slowly, and he peeks out from under his arm, quickly darting his gaze away.

"Her husband was the dean of the school. He walked in on us during her tutor hours. She was splayed out on her desk. I was there, about to slide in and..."

Holy shit. I'm not quite sure that needs to be voiced.

"And she got preferential treatment while you were asked to go." *Who would ever guess this tender, vulnerable soul was hiding under all the cheesy lines and bravado?* "I'm so sorry, Finn." I paint his chest with kisses over his heart. His beautiful heart.

"There are eight of us kids. My two older brothers were already through uni or almost done. But the younger ones didn't need to suffer for my mistake. I was young and dumb, flattered by her attention, and thought I was untouchable." He shrugs and lets his arm fall to the pillow. "The whole thing freaked me out. The dean said it was a good thing we'd not actually done the deed yet. Said he'd have called the constable. Just seemed a better idea to not take that step until I found someone worth the risk."

My heart melts when he reaches up and tucks a lock of hair behind my ear. "So the girls you've taken home, you didn't...?"

"I didn't. That's not so say that I don't have other skills." He gives me a cocky smile before turning serious again. "I'm not proud of what happened in Dublin or the aftermath. Thank you for not judging me." His knuckles trail lightly down my shoulder and across the swell of my boobs smashed against his chest.

"We all have shit to deal with, and how we deal with it is up to the individual. It would be crazy for me to judge," I scoff, sliding my hand down his abdomen, making him squirm as I trace the V of his muscles.

"Like this?" Finn runs a finger down the bridge of my nose, tapping my silver septum ring. "And this?" he asks, grabbing a fistful of my hair, tugging my head to the side. He kisses me, licking at the seam of my lips before wrapping his free arm around me and pulling me closer.

"Some people wear their hearts on their sleeves. I change my hair with my mood, and nothing pisses my dad off more." The light, easy kisses I trail up his neck flames and smolders into a passionate thing that runs away from us.

"Tell me what you said earlier." I lazily stroke his cock, running a finger around just below the crown.

He groans and gently thrusts his hips. Scooting down his body, I slide my leg across his hips and straddle his thighs.

Not needing any encouragement, Finn reaches into my drawer and grabs another condom, tearing open the packet. He hands me the condom and tosses me a Finn wink. "It was sexy as fuck, watching you sheath my cock. Do it again?"

I take the condom, arching a brow at him, waiting.

"Fine. I was counting in Gaelic, trying to distract myself so that I wouldn't blow too quickly."

With the lightest touch possible, I slowly roll the condom down his length. Finn watches me with hooded eyes.

"Then, I got distracted and went with whiskey, your tits, and the different colors you've had your hair." He runs his hands up my hips until he's cupping my boobs, pinching and rolling my nipples in the same lazy way I stroke him.

I lift my hips, positioning him at my entrance. "What else did you say?" I ask on a gasp as I lower myself until I'm completely and deliciously full.

Finn thrusts slow and deep, our bodies rocking, hands caressing and touching. He pulls me down, so we're chest-to-chest, the new angle robbing me of my ability to breathe.

"I said, 'You are lovely.'" He slowly drags his cock out until we're just barely connected. "That you take my breath away." He murmurs against the shell of my ear as he thrusts back in, "And that you are my heaven."

"More..." Dear God, his words squeeze at my heart.

He wraps me in a mixture of Gaelic and English as he brings me to a shattering release.

25

"Can you imagine if someone wrote you a list of reasons they loved you?"
"No. It would probably be the shortest list in the world."
"You're right. All it would say is, Everything."

Finn

I pull on the soft gray T-shirt I had done up for today. It's not a holiday, nothing special to the rest of the world. Just to me.

"Finn, you're working tonight, right?"

I quickly slide into a button-up as Addie exits the bathroom in a cloud of vanilla-scented steam. The blue of her hair is so much darker when it's wet and twisted into the complicated braid that I can't quite figure out, no matter how many times I unravel it.

I pull the sides of my shirt together, buttoning over the letters first. "I am. Will you keep me company for a bit?"

Addie slides her hands round my waist and pushes up onto her toes to kiss me. This is dangerous because there is nothing I want more than to deepen this kiss and take her back to bed, losing myself in her.

Addie breaks our kiss and nods. "Yeah, I have to get some work done though. What time are you going in?" She sifts through the few bits of clothing she keeps at my flat.

I've not moved yet, but I did talk with my landlord about his daughter breaking in. He installed a keypad lock for us instead, and I've not seen Bitchy McCuntface around the pub in ages.

"Erm...I have some things to get done before my shift, and Kieran needs to leave early again. I should probably go soon."

"Again?" She spins, hands on her hips. "What the hell does he do? He's never at work on time. Never works a whole shift. Why does Francie keep him?"

"The accent, love. He's got it, and he can pour a pint. I'll get him sorted."

Addie rolls her eyes and plops down on my bed, shoving her foot into a red Converse. "That's stupid. If he can't show up and do the whole job completely, then he needs to be replaced. There should be ramifications for not..." She's lost in her head and mumbling about McBride's.

She's so fucking cute; I can hardly stand it. With all the stealth I can manage, I tackle her to the bed, caging her in and kissing her until her hands are pulling at my belt, and we're both panting.

"I have to go, Addie. But I promise you, we'll pick this up later, yeah?" I drop a last kiss to her thoroughly swollen lips and climb off the bed, tucking my erection away the best that I can. Then, I head to McBride's as she goes back to her flat.

Adelaide

Finn is up to something. He thinks he can hide shit from me and have all the surprises, but I have a few of my own.

I didn't lie to him when I said I had work to do today. I have several new clients and have been busier than ever. Nope, I didn't lie. I just didn't tell him the whole truth.

Aidan has been outrageously generous in handing out my name, recommending my work, and the inquiries have been shocking, to say the least. Through his photo shoots with several bands and ever-expanding client list, I've been hired to overhaul the website and promo materials for one of the big music festivals in Kansas City.

Timing has been weird, and the organizers had some issues with some of the bands and their branding, but in a show of good faith, they gave me a pair of tickets and are flying me and a guest out next week. We don't just get to attend the show; we have full access to the venue, the musicians, and an amazing setup in my hometown.

It took all of a minute for me to decide who my plus-one would be. Finn's mild obsession with music and specifically Of the Room made it a no-brainer. That, and he's weaseled his way into my cold, dead heart.

Things are all cleared with his boss for me to steal Finn away for a few days.

Back at my apartment, I set Eric down, and he scampers off to find the Flounder toy Finn gave him. I make my way to my bedroom to finish getting ready, drying my hair and styling it in soft, beachy waves. It reminds me of ocean waves, and I love it, but it might be time for another change. *Maybe purple? Maybe the soft pastel rainbow that Finn sent me for my Pinterest board?*

I swipe on mascara and some lip stain and swap out my total nerd glasses for cute nerd glasses.

Grabbing my laptop, I settle on the couch to print off the flight vouchers and festival info, making mental notes of a few major things I want to completely change on the website and a few other cool touristy things that are must-dos in Kansas City.

After a couple of hours of work, it's time. I take Eric out to do his thing, pop him into his crate, and change into the shirt Virginia scored for me. I text her on the way to my car to make sure everything is all set for Finn's surprise at McBride's.

Francie

I settle into my usual seat at the corner of the bar, waiting for the show. Neither Finn nor Adelaide has any idea of the other's surprise. Maybe an inkling that there is one, but by no means what it is.

It settles my heart to see the boy find his way, and Adelaide is good for him. He needs someone to challenge him, keep him in line, and keep his head from getting too big. He's grown up a lot in the time he's been at McBride's. Training up the new lad, Kieran, has been a challenge— one that Jimmy wasn't quite up to and didn't manage nearly as well as I'd hoped. But Finn's got him sorted. I have all the faith in the world that Finn will be able to sort Jimmy out as well, if need be.

Applying to the university for his business classes was the final little step the boy needed to get himself lined up for the future. He needed to put the events from Dublin behind him. Know that he's capable of taking the courses he'll need to run a business. To secure his future. Because, as much as I love all my boys here—Aidan, Jimmy, Finn, and now, Kieran—there is only one completely suited to take over when the time comes.

Finn has a love for McBride's in a way the others don't quite possess. He loves the patrons, loves the lifestyle. It's the perfect fit for him to carry on, looking out for the boys here now, for the Irish lads along the way who need a place to land for a bit, and for himself to grow into who he's meant to be.

He'll do well.

Finn hustles through the pub, getting the last little details set. Making sure that his ladies have what they need. They are all wearing their matching shirts, newly altered to add an additional line of text, and drinking whiskey like only classy women can. Neat.

I lean in as he comes back to the bar. "Make sure the grannies have a round on me, yeah?"

He gives me a sly look and asks, "Want me to put that on your tab, old man?" He sets a fresh pint of Guinness in front of me and winks.

I check the clock above the bar. "It's about time."

Finn looks over his shoulder, and with a quick nod, he pulls his button-up shirt over his head, leaving him in just the T-shirt he's so proud of.

An outrageous smile stretches across my face as Adelaide makes her way through the door. The air stills as she searches the dark interior, looking a little unsure until her eyes adjust and her gaze lands on Finn. The dramatic gobshite plants his hands on the bar top and hops over it to get to her, unwilling to wait the seconds it would take to walk the twenty or so feet.

"So, you're on board with the ladies." He nods to the round table in the center of the room after taking in Adelaide's #TeamFinn shirt.

Adelaide shrugs and runs a finger across his own shirt emblazoned with #TeamAddie in pinks, greens, and blues. "I like this." She looks up at him, her smile matching his. "So, this is it? This relationship is officially defined?"

"It is," he answers with just as much cheek.

He pulls the tickets he bought for them to go to a concert in Kansas City from his pocket. The same tickets that she has in a packet for him.

These two are meant for each other as much as Aidan and Lis are. Gracyn will find her man when she stops trying to hide from the truth of who she is.

All in all, these people are my family. My boys and their ladies, my girls and their men.

Sometimes, you hold tight to the secrets that need to be kept.

For love. For life. For the best.

Thank you for spending time in Beekman Hills with Finn and Addie. I would love to know what you think of these two! If you can, please drop a quick review on your favorite retailer for me!

To stay up on releases and happenings, make sure you're signed up for my newsletter at www.kcenderswrites.com

...now, jump into **Tombstones** to meet Jack and Kate, or **Troubles** for more Aidan and Lis.

If it's Gracyn's story you're looking for, grab **In Tune** (formerly Tunes).

ALSO BY KC ENDERS

Sign up for my newsletter at www.kcenderswrites.com for release alerts

Beekman Hills Series

Troubles

Twist

Tombstones

Stand Alone Titles

Sweet on You

Broken: A Salvation Society Novel

The UnBroken Series

In Tune *(formerly Tunes)*

Off Bass

Coming Soon

Beat Down

Out Loud

ACKNOWLEDGMENTS

Twist was never supposed to be a thing. I had no intention of writing Finn's story; he was strictly a side character. Sweet and goofy, loyal and protective, but just out for a good time. This wasn't supposed to happen. But sometimes life takes a left turn and you need something light and fun to take your mind off the serious life changes going on in your world. This little project provided me with a break, the laughter and goofiness I needed more than anything. For that, I will forever be grateful to my friend, Finn.

I just hope I didn't ruin things at McBride's! Once a flirt, always a flirt, so, ladies, don't stop teasing him—

Christy Wallingford, without you, this would have never happened! You deserve the biggest thank you there is for this. You held my hand, patted my head, brainstormed, laughed, and snorted with me for countless hours through this crazy little side project and brought Finn to life.

Marisol Scott and Kate Spitzer, thank you for reading, laughing, and adding to the ridiculousness of Finn. The idea started with a comment in McBride's and grew and grew until it couldn't be contained. Thank you for all of your amazing support.

Boy #1 and the infamous Sparky, thank you for having those cheesy pickup lines at the ready. Boy #1 and I were chatting at our taproom—Cinder Block Brewery, in North Kansas City—and I mentioned needing more pickup lines. He whipped out his phone, texted his friend Sparky and the response was so fast, my head spun! Thank you, love. I hope they work better for you than they did for Finn! ...maybe Sparky needs a book...

Boy #2, your time is coming. Ideas are being discussed.

Thank you to the ladies of McBride's who can't seem to wait to get their hands on Finn, your support and enthusiasm has been AMAZING!

And to my Tribe, my author friends, the bloggers, and readers who always go above and beyond in encouragement, support, and promotion, THANK YOU! You all make me life so full.

ABOUT THE AUTHOR

KC Enders

Karin is a New York Girl living in a Midwest world. A connoisseur of great words, fine bourbon, and strong coffee, she's married to the love of her life and is mother to two grown men that she is proud to say can cook and clean up after themselves, and always open doors for the ladies thanks to the Rules of Being a Gentleman (you're welcome, world).
Her one major vice is rescuing and adopting big dogs.
Tons of personality, not so good on manners.
She loves talking books, hearing from readers, and hosting the occasional virtual
Happy Hour in her reading group.

www.kcenderswrites.com

Made in the USA
Monee, IL
22 July 2023